This book is
You may renew
You car
visit

CEN
569

DARK ANGEL RIDING

John Dancer was a drifter. He came upon a young woman weeping after raiders had lynched her husband and taken everything from their ranch. Dancer was compelled to help Cassie Blythe, but he was up against a web of deceit and murder on the range. Then the raiders returned with guns blazing and John was shot to pieces. But Dancer was determined to return to face the raiders — and vowed to even the score as a dark angel riding.

LOGAN WINTERS

DARK ANGEL RIDING

Complete and Unabridged

LINFORD
Leicester

First published in Great Britain in 2007 by
Robert Hale Limited
London

First Linford Edition
published 2009
by arrangement with
Robert Hale Limited
London

British Library CIP Data

Winters, Logan
    Dark angel riding.—Large print ed.—
    Linford western library
    1. Western stories
    2. Large type books
    I. Title
    823.9'14 [F]

    ISBN 978–1–84782–511–7

Published by
F. A. Thorpe (Publishing)
Anstey, Leicestershire

Set by Words & Graphics Ltd.
Anstey, Leicestershire
Printed and bound in Great Britain by
T. J. International Ltd., Padstow, Cornwall

1

From his upstairs window in the Brownsville Hotel, John Dancer looked out across the whitesand desert, watching the shadows beneath the thorny ocotillo plants and scattered mesquite bushes stretch out before the glare of orange light cast by the rising sun. A mockingbird perched briefly on his window ledge, cocked a surprised head at him and quickly flew away, its throat filled with scolding sounds.

Dancer smiled faintly and returned to his rumpled bed where he sat for a long minute staring at the blank wall of the room, the white pitcher and washbasin on the bureau, the clouded oval mirror which reflected only another blank wall.

He looked with a pang of trepidation at his boots, dreading the moment. He had been wearing only soft moccasins on his feet for a long while. Now his sturdy, scuffed boots presented a significant challenge. He had risen in the early pre-dawn hours and managed, with infinite care and spasms of pain to dress himself in the faded red shirt and black jeans he now wore. Each movement caused jagged torment to flare up in his tightly wrapped ribcage. The broken bones were nearly mended, but they violently objected to any movement that was not carefully planned, gently executed.

Dancer had no choice but to move on. He had been staying in the hotel for two months now, half the time flat on his back; now his funds were exhausted. If he was careful with his few remaining dollars he had enough to provision himself, pay for his horse's board and stock his saddlebags with enough ammunition to do what must be done.

Broken, his body was still unwilling, but his spirit raced with fiery determination. Two months is a long time to remain a dead man. It was time to return.

With a sigh, he leaned to pick up his left boot. His ribs complained again at the small exertion. Dancer cursed the demons of pain to silence. Tugging at the mule-ear straps he drew his calf-high boot on. The easy part, then, had been accomplished. Now he morosely studied the other boot, and then his swollen, shattered right foot. On either side of the ankle was a knob where displaced bone had reconstructed itself grotesquely. The doctor who had strapped him into his encasing rib bandages had examined the deformed ankle and shaken his head. 'It'll never be any good again,' was the physician's unnecessary prognosis.

'Amazing what a .44-40 slug can do to the human body,' the youngish doctor said. 'Tendon, bone, flesh.' He was not callous, but only candid. 'You'll never walk again, Mr Dancer. Not without extreme pain.'

'I'll ride, then,' Dancer had told the

physician with stony certainty. The young doctor's eyes flickered behind his spectacles as he studied the expression on his lanky, curly-headed patient's face. 'There's places I have to go,' Dancer told him. 'I'll get there if I have to crawl.'

The doctor, a mild man from the East, saw the fire in Dancer's faded blue eyes and began wrapping the swollen, broken ankle. He believed Dancer. Believed he would be able to do whatever it was that he had planned, and was glad that he himself was not going to be standing in John Dancer's way.

Now Dancer delayed. He wiped back his dark hair with the fingers of both hands, took a deep breath and thrust the toes of his foot into his boot. As he gripped the straps perspiration began to bead his forehead. He stifled a cry of pain as he tugged steadily, strongly at the boot, watching the swollen, mis-shapen object that was his ankle slide into his boot, inch by tormenting inch until, rising, he silently groaned and stamped his foot down hard, his heel settling into the boot.

Then he slumped back onto the bed, the throb and ache searing through his ankle, the whole of his left leg. A soft rap on his door brought Dancer instantly upright and he snatched his Colt revolver from the bureau top, easing back the blue-steel hammer.

'Who is it?' Dancer asked in a low growl.

'Me, Sadie, Mr Dancer.'

Dancer lowered the hammer of the Colt and hobbled to the door. Upon opening it he found the tiny chestnut-haired maid who had taken care of him these last long weeks. Sadie Fairchild stood at the threshold of the room, towels folded over her arm, a steaming bucket of hot water in her free hand. Her dark eyes were inquisitive, growing anxious as she studied John Dancer from his freshly washed dark hair to the tight-fitting high boots he now wore.

'I came for your soak,' she said, a

slight tremor in her voice. 'But I see . . . '

'Come on in,' Dancer said, leaving the door open as she passed him and placed the bucket of water on the floor, the towels on the bureau. Beyond the window the sky was losing its dawn tint, fading to a clear blue-white. Sadie remained standing, her arms crossed beneath her breasts.

'I guess they didn't tell you,' Dancer said. 'I'm leaving this morning.'

'They didn't tell me,' Sadie replied softly.

Since the night John Dancer had dragged himself into the hotel and taken a room, Sadie Fairchild had been tending to his needs. Each morning she brought a bucket of hot water to pour into the basin so that John could soak his damaged ankle. When he needed meals delivered, mail sent, aspirin or — occasionally — whiskey to dampen his pain, she cheerfully provided these services.

Sometimes at night she would read to

him, seated in a wooden chair beside the bed where the wounded man lay, her voice tender and low. Though he did not know it, at times Sadie would sit and watch him sleep, long after the book had been closed and the night crept past, stroking his forehead when the occasional nightmare swam through his unconscious mind.

'Is it money, John?' she asked, studying him intently. He had unintentionally mentioned to her that his funds were nearly exhausted. 'If that is all it is, I can . . . '

Dancer waved a careless hand. 'It's not that, Sadie. It's just that it's time to go. I have matters to attend to.'

'Your foot is no better!' she said with impulsive heat.

'I can ride.'

'You can be killed,' Sadie said, her voice lowering. She shifted her eyes away from his. They had spoken together for long hours over the months; they knew more than they needed to know about each other's troubles.

Sadie Fairchild had been only a child when her family, trekking westward, had been raided by a band of Comanches west of Brownsville. Through a small miracle she had been left alive, lost and hungry, fearful and small on the wide prairie until discovered by an army patrol. The owners of the hotel, Guy Travers and his wife, Tess, had taken the orphaned child in. Sadie had remained in their service for years. She found that she feared the wide land deeply and could never again even consider venturing out onto the empty plains. Also, her devotion to Guy Travers — shark though he was — and to Tess, was unshakeable. She was their child, they the only parents she had known.

'A lot of men,' Sadie tried again as Dancer belted on his Colt revolver, bracing himself heavily on his left leg, 'live full lives, rewarding lives without guns. Without carving a path into Hell.'

Dancer didn't quite smile. There was nothing amusing about Sadie's words or her fear, but the corners of his broad mouth did lift slightly as he responded.

'You're right, of course. You are a wise woman, Sadie.' Somberly, he added, 'But when a man is given no choice, he will charge Hell with a pocketful of stones if he must. Or he relinquishes the right to call himself a man.'

'You mustn't do this . . . ' *to me*, is what she nearly blurted out, but refrained from saying. She performed meaningless habitual rituals now as she kept her moist eyes turned away from Dancer's — opening the window, stripping the bed of its linen, straightening the braided rug at the foot of the bed. When none of these small distractions could longer disguise her fear, she spun to face Dancer and said furiously:

'For God's sake, John! She is only another woman!'

Immediately she regretted her outburst. John Dancer seemed not to have heard her. He was packing his few belongings into his saddlebags, not so much as glancing at her. Sadie felt diminished, as if her outburst had shrunken her in his eyes, made her sound like another jealous female — jealous about a woman she had never met or seen, described only through Dancer's eyes on those long, quiet, somehow comforting nights when she had seated herself close to him, wanting to know him, to find an anchor, a polar star in her life beyond the security of the Travers family.

Sadie felt at once rejected and, as one who has made a fool of herself, as causing her own rejection.

John Dancer said, 'Have Guy make up my bill, and if you could send young Toby to the stable for my horse . . . ' He fumbled in his pocket for a pair of silver dollars to offer her, saw that even that gesture was offensive to Sadie, and let his words stumble to a halt.

'I wasn't meaning to treat you like . . . '

'A servant?' Sadie suggested. But that

was all that she had been to John Dancer, it seemed now. Dancer didn't reply. 'I'll send Toby for your gray,' she promised. Moving like an automaton now, Sadie gathered her pail and towels and started toward the door. Dancer took her arm in passing, turned her and held her briefly by the shoulders, searching for words. None came. This time had passed — all too quickly, but it had passed. They dwelt in different worlds; they had different expectations.

'Please let me go,' she said without raising her eyes to Dancer's. He released his hands slowly and watched as she trudged purposefully down the carpeted hallway. Dancer's mouth tightened with emotions he refused to pause to define, and he returned to the room stiffly to plant his gray Stetson on his head, look around briefly for forgotten items, snatch his Winchester rifle from the corner of the closet and limp down the corridor himself, saddlebags over his shoulder, his ankle throbbing with pain at each step. The boot acted as a sort of splint, preventing further damage, but Dancer doubted that he could withdraw his foot from it again without cutting the leather away. His ankle crackled and grated as he walked. His teeth, as he started down the stairway toward the lobby, were gritted.

The hotel lobby in the cool early hours was dark, musty. Two Texas cattlemen in range clothes sat sagged into overstuffed chairs, watching with whiskey-blurred eyes as Dancer walked past them. Guy Travers's small brown-and-white dog, head resting on its paws, opened one eye to watch Dancer as he approached the counter.

There was a bell on the scarred desk and, placing his rifle on the counter, he rang it. Guy Travers, smelling of bay rum and shaving soap, his white shirtsleeves held up with red garters, appeared from the back room of the office, smiling uneasily. He eyed Dancer nervously, placed both of his stubby hands on the desk and said, 'Tess is making out your bill, Mr Dancer. I'm sorry to ask you to leave before you were fully ready, but . . . ' He shrugged.

'Business is business,' Dancer said.

'I realize with your medical problems . . . '

'It was time to leave anyway,' Dancer said without a smile. He leaned against the counter, turning his eyes away from the pathetic hotel-keeper. He wondered how Sadie had managed to endure all these years in his employ. Tess Travers bustled in from the rear office, a yellow slip of paper fluttering in her hand. She was short, round and constantly harried. A woman who seemed always to be apologizing for herself . . . or for her husband. Dancer took the hotel bill and studied it. It was a dollar over what it should have been, but he wasn't going to waste the time to haggle over it.

Counting out his money, he found that he was closer to being totally broke than he had previously estimated. Travers nodded, scraped the money from the counter. Tess Travers smiled nervously and murmured, 'We hope to have you stay with us again, Mr Dancer.'

Dancer's face was expressionless. He picked up his rifle, shifted the weight of his saddlebags from one shoulder to the other and walked toward the hotel door. He would not be passing this way again.

Just before he stepped through the green door into the glitter of the desert morning he saw, from the corner of his eye, the chestnut-haired girl with those sad green eyes, watching him from a deeply shadowed corner of the lobby. Dancer stepped outside, closed the door firmly and hobbled toward the stable.

Toby Waller was a cheerful, bright-eyed kid. He wore hand-me-down shirt and trousers two sizes too large, a torn hat and a toothy grin. His shoes were scarred and misshapen, one ear was slightly folded. He was rooted in poverty, unschooled and totally affable. He rose from the water barrel he had been perched on and waited, arms akimbo, to greet Dancer in a chirruping voice.

'Mr Dancer! Sadie told me you'd be coming today!'

'And here I am,' Dancer said, resting his big hand on the boy's slender shoulder.

'I'll hate to see Washoe leave,' Toby said. 'Me and that big gray horse have had some mornings. I was just getting ready to take him out for his exercise when Miss Sadie told me you were on your way. He's fit and ready. I readjusted the stirrups for you.'

In the darkness of the stable it took a minute before Dancer's eyes adjusted well enough for him to be able to make out the familiar figure of the gray horse with three white stockings, the full chest and devilish eyes.

'He didn't give you any trouble?' Dancer said as they reached the stall where Washoe waited. Dancer stroked the big horse's muzzle.

'Naw!' Toby reconsidered, 'Well . . . he can be a little feisty in the mornings.'

'He can be,' Dancer agreed, opening the stall gate to run a hand along the tall gray's flanks. Curried and well-fed, Washoe looked to be in splendid shape.

'You didn't break a gallop on him, did you?' Dancer asked. Toby looked slightly offended.

'No, sir, Mr Dancer! You told me not to let him run flat out, and I gave you my promise.'

Dancer had slipped his rifle into its saddle sheath, now he was tying his saddlebags down.

'He looks fine, Toby. I thank you.' He fished into his pocket and pulled out a silver dollar which he gave to the boy.

'I almost feel bad about taking this,' Toby said gazing at the cartwheel. 'Mornings I couldn't wait to get to work when Washoe was here. Now . . . '

'Have you got a stool, Toby? The kind some of these young ladies need to climb aboard?'

'For you, sir?' Toby asked with disbelief.

'For me. I'm just a little game still,'

Dancer answered.

Washoe did not act up on this morning, perhaps sensing his master's difficulty. Once in leather, the pain in Dancer's ankle settled to a slow throb. It was from horseback that he paid the stablekeeper what was owed for his horse's care. Then, ducking his head, Dancer rode out into the sun-bright street, slowly walked Washoe up the center of Main Street, the gray's prancing hoofs kicking up small puffs of white sandy dust. Past the saloons, past the restaurant, past the gunsmith's. Past the hotel and along the length of the street until it faded, broadened and disappeared, merging with the endless salt flats of the long white desert.

The morning was already warm. By noon the temperature would be in three figures. At The Wells, just beyond the town, he paused. There were several Mexican women in striped skirts and white blouses filling *ollas* with water for their cooking and household tasks. Dancer didn't risk swinging down to fill his canteens. Instead he gave one of the women a few pesos to do it for him.

This was going to be hell, he thought, as he watched a few young dark-eyed kids running, playing tag with each other, a half-dozen scrawny pups yipping at their heels. The doctor had told him he would never walk normally again. Dancer had already known that — had known it as soon as the bullet tagged his ankle on that blazing day. A man proceeds as best he can. He could no longer walk more than a few hundred feet at a time.

But he could ride and he could shoot. He could find the killers and exact his revenge. His mood grew darker, his expression bitter as he started forward out onto the treacherous desert. He was determined, and a deadly desire for vengeance rode with him.

His ankle might be broken and useless, but it made no difference. He would descend upon the killers not like a man afoot and hobbled, but like a dark angel riding.

18

2

Three months earlier, when John Dancer had trailed into this country out of Alamogordo, it had been the dead of winter, or what passed for winter in this bleak desert country. The nights could grow bitter cold, but the daytime temperatures seldom topped the high eighties. It wasn't the blazing white sun that troubled a man at that time of year, but the sheer bleakness of the long desert, the sense that the empty land ran on to infinity.

Dancer had not known the country then, but a man named French who had once tried hard-rock mining up this way had drawn him a crude map. The low, slate-gray hills to Dancer's left were where he had expected to find them. These were rugged, folded desolate hills with only a hint of green at their peaks — probably stunted weather-tortured piñon pines. His campsite was intended to be Wildcat Canyon. If he could discover it. There, French had told him, shallow pools of water could usually be found and shelter from the not uncommon, fierce sandstorms.

The day on which it had all begun lived in vivid recollection . . .

★ ★ ★

The sun, low in the western sky, spread a rose-colored flush across the white sand. The dusk had been rushing toward darkness; there was a last line of beaten gold along the formless horizon and a smear of burnt orange in the higher sky mixed with hazy vermilion. The horse was weary, moving with its head down, plodding through the sand and scattered volcanic rock.

Cresting out a low rise, Dancer heard the keening sound, and he frowned, slowing his gray horse still more. 'What was that, Washoe?' Dancer asked quietly. 'Didn't sound like coyotes.' It didn't sound like any cry that he could remember hearing. Indians? He thought the Yaquis and the Yuma Indians were not found this far north and east, but of course he couldn't risk being wrong.

He unsheathed his Winchester rifle and kneed the big gray horse forward. On the far side of the rise he heard the sound once more and his eyes searched the sundown-colored land intently. Then he saw the *thing*.

In a grassless hollow below where he sat his pony, he saw it backlighted by the orange sky. It was a dark, ominous form, swinging from the end of a rope looped over the branch of a lone broken cottonwood tree. The thing was not making the sound, for the thing could not. The hanged man was no longer capable of moaning, of movement or thought.

But the sound did shiver across the desert once more, and as Dancer slowly walked Washoe forward, the horse's hoofs whishing faintly through the inches-deep sand, he saw the other figure. The dead man hung dark and motionless against the sky from the noose fixed around his neck. At his feet knelt a hooded creature.

It was a woman, her hands to her face, her body trembling with sorrow or fear, perhaps a combination of these. She heard the horse's approaching hoofs and her face, ghostly white, drawn by stark fear, spun toward Dancer. She made to rise, got tangled in her hooded robe and collapsed against the sand, moaning softly.

Dancer swung down from the horse and walked to her, leading Washoe.

'Just kill me!' the woman said from her prostrate position. 'Do whatever you want to do. I have nothing to live for any more!'

'You've got me wrong,' Dancer said. His twilight shadow was long across her huddled form. 'I just want to help you if you need help.'

One eye flickered open and the woman peered up at John Dancer.

'You're not one of them?'

'I'm not one of anything,' Dancer said. 'Just someone who wandered into your trouble, whatever it is. Who is this man to you?' he asked, lifting his chin toward the hanging man.

'My husband . . . he was . . . ' She seemed incapable of further speech.

'All right. You don't want to leave him hanging here, I know. What do you want to do?'

Shaking uncontrollably, the woman sat up. She attempted to dust the dirt from her cowled robe with her trembling hands, and answered, keeping her eyes averted from the dangling shadow: 'I just want to take him home. To bury him properly,' she said.

'All right, then. Let's do that,' Dancer said, crouching. His broad mouth formed a smile of compassion. 'Where do you live?'

'There,' she said, pointing toward the valley below them where willows and cottonwood trees crowded what appeared to be a stream bank. 'Our house is just beyond the trees.'

The spot she indicated was no more than a quarter of a mile away. Dancer frowned, peering into the dusk-clad distances, unable to see a structure there. Rising from his crouch, he told the woman:

'All right, then. Let's get you home. You can ride my horse. I can shoulder your husband that far.' The woman eyed Washoe as if the horse were a fearsome beast.

'No,' she said. 'I'll walk. I can show you the way.'

Dancer didn't argue. He nodded, turned Washoe, and as the woman rose from the ground, he removed his skinning-knife from its boot sheath, placed his right boot in the left stirrup and rose to grip the hanging rope, cutting through it in two precise strokes. The dead body fell to the earth with the sound of a sandbag dropping. The young woman turned her head away and placed her hands to her face again.

'Start on, if you like,' Dancer told her. 'I'll catch up.'

The woman walked away through the purple murk of evening as Dancer braced himself and hefted the dead man. Washoe was unhappy with the task, but held his station as John flopped the dead body across the gray's neck. The big horse shied slightly, but was calmed by Dancer's reassuring words and strokes of his neck. Dancer swung easily aboard and, after a deep breath, started Washoe after the lonely desert woman as twilight darkened to bleak, featureless night.

Leaving the trees which lined the night-darkened river, they came to a low-roofed house of sawn lumber. It was neater than Dancer had expected to find out here on the desert. The country around was not all sandy wilderness, for he distinctly smelled grass and livestock, though he could see neither horses nor cattle in the settling darkness. The moon was still only a vague promise below the horizon.

They had water, and some graze here, but whether the ranch was a prosperous one, he could not tell. The house was only a modest indicator of wealth. Dancer had seen ranches of 5,000 acres and more run from such small dwellings. And, even though many in this part of the country owned thousands upon thousand of acres, there was not enough rainfall to provide grass for many animals.

The woman waited on the porch as Dancer, the body of the dead man slung over Washoe's neck, approached and reined up. There was no lamp lit inside the house — where were the ranch hands, if any? Who was the dead man? A convicted killer or a lynched rancher of good standing? Dancer had come to the woman's aid because she was alone and in need of help, but he had to wonder what situation he might unwarily have blundered into.

Dancer swung down from Washoe and tried to meet the woman's eyes in the near-darkness. Behind her, *ollas* containing water hung on heavy cords from the eaves and strings of drying red chilli peppers — common in this part of the country. All seemed usual, ordinary. Except for the dead man draped across Washoe's withers.

'I'll need a shovel, ma'am . . . if you would show me where he . . . should be put.'

'There's a toolshed around the corner of the house,' the woman said with a weary wave of her hand. 'There's a lone oak tree standing just beyond it. Aaron would have liked it there, I believe.' Her words rushed on. 'I'll be inside the house; I can't watch. I will start some coffee boiling.'

Dancer frowned. The woman's mood seemed to change abruptly from moment to moment, but then sudden death can spawn bewilderment. It was best for her, best for him, to take care of the job at hand as soon as possible. Leading a skittish Washoe, Dancer made his way around the corner of the house, found the toolshed and the oak tree, now black against the starry sky, and got to work.

* * *

Heat still rose from the sand even at this late hour to linger in the starbright sky until a new morning arrived. Beyond the serried hills the full moon peered cautiously, casting moon shadows beneath the scattered sage and mesquite. Having tucked the pick and shovel he had used away in the toolshed, Dancer slowly buttoned his shirt and walked back to the front of the white house, leading Washoe.

He had no idea what to say to the woman: there was nothing to be said. She astonished him by appearing in the back-lighted doorway holding a mug of coffee for him. She had removed her cloak and hood, and stood revealed in a light summer dress of white with tiny blue rosebuds stitched into it. She had obviously taken the time to wash her face and brush her long blond hair. If this had been their first meeting he would have taken her for a pleasant, well-groomed, attentive hostess, not a troubled young window.

Her smile failed to support her façade. It trembled, welcoming without beckoning. Dancer looped his horse's reins over the sagging hitch rail, and approached her, hat in hand.

'I can't thank you enough for . . . ' she said in a near whisper.

'No need to,' John Dancer answered, accepting the coffee cup she extended to him.

'Come in for a minute,' she said, nervously. 'Sit for a while.'

'All right. If you don't mind,' he replied, crossing the comfortable front room with its braided rug and two identical leather sofas. On the wall above a native-stone fireplace a grizzly bear head's glass eyes gazed solemnly down. The kitchen was wider than the living room, as befitted a ranch house where a dozen hands might linger around the dinner table. A few poor wild flowers — blue lupines and black-eyed Susans — in a ceramic vase at the center of the table drooped their weary heads.

'Sit down,' the woman said. Unusually, she did not offer the wanderer food as was the custom in the Far country, but this had been no usual day for her.

Dancer sat, placing his hat on the table. The woman stood aside, hands folded together. Tentatively she spoke. 'You were just passing by?'

'Yes, ma'am. As I told you.'

'You were headed . . . ?'

'I don't know for sure. But it's round-up time and someone can always use an extra hand or two. I've a friend named Ned French down in Alamogordo. He told me that there are plenty of boot-strap ranchers trying to make a go of it a little north of you.' He shrugged. 'I figured to try my luck up there.'

'*In that case,*' a low voice from behind Dancer said, 'I suggest you get on your horse now and trail out of here.

I wouldn't want you to lose a job.'

There were two of them standing in the doorway behind John Dancer. The front door had been left open to the cooling night and they had slipped in quietly as he talked to the widow. Friends, foes, murderers or protectors of the young woman, he did not know and could not guess. The woman took a half-step forward and said:

'Jared! He helped me.'

'You won't be needing his help any longer. We're back,' the man called Jared told her.

Dancer still had not turned his head to glance at the men whose presence was only announced by their voices and by the long shadows that crossed the kitchen floor. He kept his hand wrapped around the coffee mug, not wanting to give the wrong impression by any sudden move. These people had their reasons for mistrust. Whatever they were, he had no further interest in their business now that the hanged man had been buried.

'I'll be reaching for my hat,' Dancer said softly. 'Then I'll be on my way.'

'Hold it!' the second man said. By his shadow Dancer saw that he was narrower, taller than Jared. 'What's your name, stranger?'

'John. Some down home call me Jack.'

'Where's home?' the thin man inquired.

Dancer admitted with a thin smile, 'Alamogordo lately. But mostly where I hang my hat and can sit to a table and have my dinner.'

'Just a drifter?' Jared demanded.

'That about covers it,' Dancer answered mildly.

* * *

Dancer saw the two men's shadows briefly merge, heard a whispered exchange. Then the two men withdrew, Jared reminding him: 'Just sit where you are. Don't make a move. We've got you in our sights.'

Dancer had no intention of moving. It is not a feasible course of action when you have two men with guns drawn at your back. He lifted his eyes instead to the young blonde woman across the table. She showed no signs of fear, but her eyes were thinly sheened with moisture.

'They don't seem to like me,' Dancer said lightly, hoping for a smile, but the girl only shook her head.

'It's their way,' she told him.

Dancer could hear the two, now withdrawn into the living room, speaking in low voices, but he could not make out their words. He sipped at his coffee — now cooled — and waited for them to return, still wondering what he had gotten himself into with his generous impulse to help the young lady, for it was certain there was some sort of trouble brewing. Men did not generally draw down on a stranger in their own house as a form of hospitality.

★   ★   ★

'We just shoo him out of here,' Jared Fine was saying. 'He's a drifter. Nothing to us.'

'Let me enlighten you,' Charley Spikes hissed back at the big man. 'I know who he is — running him off would be a big mistake.' Charley dragged his fingers through his unruly dark beard and, goaded by Jared's inquisitive eyes, finally told him: 'That's John Dancer! Didn't you hear him.'

'Dancer?' Jared searched his memory. He shook his head heavily. 'Don't know of him.'

'You would if you'd spent time in New Mexico Territory like I have. Hear him say he was up from Alamogordo? Well, that's where I saw him, Jared,' Spikes said, growing more excited. He had his cocked revolver in his hand still, his eyes occasionally darting to the open kitchen door. The narrow, bearded man went on:

'He's a well-known gun down that way. I never seen him work, but I know what people were saying.'

Jared scratched his shoulder, frowning. 'Won't he know you, then? Know that we're onto him.'

'We were never exactly introduced. Besides,' Charley said, tugging at his chin-whiskers, 'I didn't have this brush on my face back then.'

'I don't like it much,' Jared said hesitating.

'You'll like it less if he hooks up with LaFrance and Luke Gamer,' Charley Spikes advised him. 'You heard what Dancer said — he's just looking for work. I say we hire him on.'

'What makes you think he'll listen to us?'

'It's not us he'll listen to,' Charley replied slyly. 'But he will listen to Cassandra. What man wouldn't?'

Jared half-turned and his eyes briefly met Cassandra Blythe's across the distance. Young, pretty, a distraught new widow . . . yes, Dancer would listen to her. Any man would. They just had to convince her of their reasons. With a sigh, Jared told Charley Spikes,

'It only makes sense to take on another fighting man.'

Holstering their revolvers they re-entered the kitchen together, this time walking around the table to face Dancer from behind Cassandra. It was Jared who spoke.

'I'm sorry, John. As you must have noticed, we've had some trouble lately. Seeing you, we just sort of flew off the handle, not knowing who you were, or maybe if you'd been bothering Cassie here.'

'He only helped me,' Cassandra said, glancing up at Jared.

'Yeah, well, we see that now,' Jared Fine said, tilting back his greasy hat. 'But coming into the house so soon after they lynched Aaron . . . we were a little jittery, you understand?'

'I think so,' Dancer said equably.

'If you are looking for work,' Jared went on, 'we could use another man around the place — especially now. That is if Cassie is agreeable.'

The small woman's eyes flashed with

a ferocity Dancer couldn't have imagined, even stronger than the look she had given him at the site of the lynching. Her teeth barely unclenched as she leveled her gaze at John Dancer. 'We need men, that's right,' she said with fire. 'We need men who will fight for the brand. If you're not willing, John, then I don't want you around. They've started a war, and you've dropped into the middle of it.'

Dancer turned his cup in his hands and nodded distantly. His own cool blue eyes met Cassandra Blythe's. He asked her:

'Where do I bunk down?'

★   ★   ★

The bunk house was a long, low structure of unbarked logs visible just beyond the willow brush and cottonwood trees that fronted the river. It was full dark as Dancer, having put his horse up in the barn, walked toward the building, carrying only his saddlebags and bedroll.

Stars flourished in the wide, cold sky and the narrow river caught their light and reflected it in its slow passing. An owl dived low at Dancer, perhaps protecting a nearby nest and he waved his hat at it. It sloped away on broad wings, vanishing into the desert night.

There was a low light burning at one end of the log house, but the building remained silent as Dancer approached it, rapped twice on the heavy plank door and entered. Constructed to house a dozen men, all of the bunks were now empty, the ticking-covered mattresses rolled up. At the far end of the building where the lantern burned low, Dancer saw a figure huddled beneath an army blanket.

'Hey there!' Dancer called out. Then he walked that way, boot heels clicking against the wooden floor. 'You!' he said in a quieter voice. The man beneath the blanket stirred and sat up. His hand was gripped around the butt of a Colt

Navy revolver. His eyes were deeply set, his gaunt face bristling with white whiskers.

'I don't know you,' the old man said from his bunk. He swung his bare feet to the floor and turned up the wick on the lantern, keeping his pistol leveled at Dancer.

'No, you don't. I've just hired on,' John told him.

'Who hired you?'

'Jared Fine, Spikes and the lady,' Dancer replied. 'Where do I make my bed?'

'Anywhere you like,' the man in the bunk said, rubbing his head which was frosted with thinning white hair. 'Sorry about pulling my weapon on you,' he told Dancer. 'We've had a deal of trouble lately.'

'I know. I just buried Aaron Blythe.'

'I knew they'd kill him if they got the chance,' the old man said sadly.

'Who are they?'

'LaFrance, Luke Gamer and them over on Pinetree,' the man said waving a weary hand. 'It's a shame and a pity,' he added after a moment's sad reflection. 'Aaron Blythe was a good man'

Dancer had been busy unrolling his blanket, stuffing his saddlebags and assorted goods under the bunk three spaces down from the old man's. 'Range war, is it?' he asked, seating himself.

'What else in this part of the country? The only reason we haven't had an all-out shooting war is LaFrance and them are letting our boys do the work for them, rounding up the strays, gathering the herd before we drive them over to Carson City.'

'Is that where everybody is?' Dancer asked indicating the empty blinks. 'Out on round-up?'

'Yes,' the old man said with a tired drawl. 'There's three line shacks scattered about in the hills. The boys are up there.'

'I see.' Dancer stood to unbuckle his gun and the old cowhand studied him closely. After hanging his belt on the wall, Dancer retrieved oil, a rag and round brass brush from his goods. He shook the cartridges from his revolver and sat cleaning it.

'Use that pistol much?' the old man asked narrowly.

'Not if I can help it, Mr . . . '

'Foley,' the old-timer provided.

'I had a long ride,' John told him, continuing with his task. 'Bound to have picked up a lot of trail dust.'

Foley said, 'I appreciate seeing a man take care of his goods. When I was working down in West Texas, I seen a lot of hands, kids really, wearing their guns for nothing but show. In all weather, I mean. Dust, rain and snow. I seen men with pistols that were practically rusted shut. What good is a tool — any tool — that isn't ready for use when you need it?'

'I agree,' Dancer said. Foley seemed to be waiting for him to expand on the subject, but he didn't. Placing the rag and brush aside, Dancer reloaded his pistol, snapped the cylinder shut and hung it in its holster.

'See you got a cut-out for your trigger finger in that holster of yours.'

'You're an observant man,' was all Dancer said, pulling the boots off of his saddle-weary feet.

'I guess you'll survive out here longer than most,' Foley said, curling up again in his blanket, turning his back to Dancer.

'What do you mean?' John asked.

'Nothing,' the muffled voice from beneath the blanket said. 'You've already seen how matters stand around here. If you've hired on, knowing that, I suppose you're willing to stay.'

'But you wouldn't recommend it?'

'Mister, I don't recommend what people should do. But if I had your youth and a good horse, I'd consider slapping spurs to it.' He sat up abruptly and without glancing again at Dancer turned down the lantern wick until the pale, smoky light it cast fizzled to golden sparks and then was extinguished by the chill desert night, leaving John Dancer to lie back on his cot, hands behind his head and wonder what he had gotten himself into this time.

3

With the first glow of morning light John Dancer dressed and walked to the door of the bunkhouse. Foley had left a pot of hot coffee on the iron stove and John held a tin cup in his hand as he peered out into the brilliant morning. Flat rays of gold pierced the spreading oak trees. Dust motes danced densely through these. A flight of doves winged toward water as the dawn lost its color and the sky paled. A yellow dog, its tail curled between its legs, slunk toward the bunkhouse, looked up at John with mistrustful brown eyes and scurried away.

Dancer had no idea where Foley had gone, nor where anyone else on the ranch might be. First things first. He collected his saddlebags and went out, tugging his hat lower. Whatever job they had in mind for him this day, he would need Washoe and so he walked toward the barn, his boots kicking up little puffs of dust. He startled a cottontail in his passing, and the small rabbit launched itself into a zigzagging run through the willow brush that fronted the river.

Inside the barn it was still cool and shadowed, horse-smelling. Three ponies stood there now, watching his approach with pricked ears. He had no idea whose animals these were, where their riders might be.

Whistling under his breath, he curried Washoe's gunmetal-colored coat, spread his striped blanket over the horse's broad back and hoisted the saddle. He cinched down the twin straps on the Texas-rigged saddle, took bridle and bit from a rusty nail on the wall of the barn and slipped Washoe into his working gear.

Before leading the horse out into the brilliant morning sunlight, he double-checked the cinches. Now and then he still ran across a man who asked him why he used a double-cinched Texas-style saddle when it was twice as much trouble. All Dancer could do was to reply with a smile, figuring the man had never roped a 1000-pound steer running at full speed. It was almost funny to watch a man lasso a cow, throw a dally around his pommel and see the single cinch break. The wide-eyed look on his face as he flew up into the air still seated on his saddle. Almost . . . if it wasn't happening to you.

Dancer swung open the heavy barn door and went out into the grassless yard.

Cassandra Blythe was there, sitting on the seat of a surrey drawn by a leggy red roan with a coat so bright it looked as if it had been burnished. He noticed the Rafter B brand on the animal's smooth flank. Dancer started toward her, leading Washoe.

''Morning, Mrs Blythe. I was about to come looking for you, for someone to tell me what they wanted me to do this morning.'

Cassandra Blythe's eyes were shadowed by the wide brim of a yellow straw hat, but they were clear and direct. 'You'll be escorting me to Potrero this morning,' she said, gathering up the reins which had been looped around the brake handle.

'What's that?' he asked.

'The nearest thing we have to a town out here,' she answered. 'You won't be of much use on the round-up right now, not knowing the boundaries or the lie of the land. Jared and Charley have ridden back out to the line camps. So you are my bodyguard for the day, John.'

'All right,' he said equably, swinging aboard Washoe. Traveling in the company of this petite blonde woman was surely a better prospect than the stink and dust of gathering a trail herd. 'Are you expecting trouble of some kind?'

'Lately you can't be sure around here,' she answered. Glancing at him once more, she snapped the reins and the roan started out of the yard, moving briskly. In silence they passed through the oak grove, angling away from the river out onto the desert. Far ahead a long row of low sawtooth mountains stood huddled in shadows against the blue-white sky. Dancer took them for the Panamint Range judging by what Ned French had described to him. Slowing her high-stepping roan horse slightly, Cassie said to Dancer:

'You don't ask many questions, do you?'

'As few as possible, if it's not my business.' He had slowed Washoe to match the gait of the roan, and they crossed the desert which was dotted with greasewood and occasional thorny mesquite side by side. The conversation was as easy as if they had been seated on a settee in her parlor.

'I do want you to keep your eyes open,' she said, looking briefly fearful.

'I intend to, Mrs Blythe.'

'Call me Cassie. Everyone else does,' she instructed, and Dancer nodded. 'What I must do this morning,' Cassie explained, 'is see that my husband's will is placed into probate.' She glanced at the small reticule on the black leather seat beside her. Presumably the purse contained legal documents. 'Lord knows what LaFrance and Garner and that Pinetree bunch might get up to now that Aaron is dead. The ranch is mine!' she said with unexpected heat. 'It will remain so. I also have the deed granting water rights to the Rafter B with me. That is to be notarized and locked up in the bank's safe.

'Without the water I have nothing,' she said, looking across the wide, pale land. 'This desert country is useless without it. You could buy a hundred acres for a nickel, but what good would it do you? Land in itself is without value — it's what the land produces that gives it its worth.'

After that short outburst, she fell silent for miles, deftly guiding the rangy red roan across the rockstrewn country, dipping down into an arroyo and scrambling up the far side until they encountered what appeared to be a wagon trail. There Cassie slowed her horse to a walk, apparently believing that they were no longer in imminent danger. John Dancer had seen no one in the distances as they had proceeded. Once a slinking coyote, and the high-soaring silhouette of a red-tailed hawk, but nothing else living.

Cresting a low, slate-colored rise strewn with larger rocks and scattered thickets of nopal cactus, Dancer now saw a small, slovenly-planned town. Situated in a white desert valley where, here and there, grew poor patches of grass and a few oaks and sycamores crowded together just beyond the rough collection of weather-beaten structures. Dancer guessed that there was a stream flowing there, perhaps an extension of the river that snaked its way across the Rafter B land.

The day was dry, the wind fitful as they trailed into the ramshackle town. A few horses and mules stood listlessly at hitch rails in front of places of business, mostly they stood as if hip shot, their weight on three legs as they dozed, moving only to twitch their ears or tails if the flies were biting.

Dancer continued to be alert. That was what he was being paid for, after all, but he saw scarcely a man on the street. The road itself was roughly graded, washboarded from usage. The store fronts on the south-facing buildings were already faded by the desert sun, many of the painted legends nearly illegible despite the fact that Potrero couldn't have been built more than twenty years earlier. Two poorly dressed boys sat in a narrow strip of hot shadow between two buildings, playing mumbletypeg while their mixed-breed black dog lay watching. The dog started to rise to its feet as they passed, decided against it and sat again. It was too much trouble to bark, it seemed, and so it simply yawned as they traveled on.

'Delightful place, isn't it?' Cassandra Blythe said, her pretty mouth drawn down.

'Where are we going?' Dancer asked.

'The bank is on our right just ahead,' she said, gesturing toward it. 'It's the only building that doesn't look as if a strong wind would take it down.'

John Dancer peered into the brilliant sunlight, seeing the low adobe-block building. There were bars on its windows as if it were a jail, and in fact the building next door was the town marshal's office as an awning-sheltered hanging plank sign proclaimed. Cassie halted her horse and, shaking her head, stepped from the surrey with Dancer's assistance. Dancer tied the roan loosely to the rail and left Washoe standing ground-hitched. The well-trained gray would never break his imaginary tethers.

'The marshal's office first,' Cassie Blythe said. 'I have to report the murder of . . . ' and then she broke down. Bowing her head, she pulled a lace-fringed handkerchief from her reticule and held it to her eyes. 'Report my husband's death. Also Marshal

52

Bingham will have to witness the execution of Aaron's will.' She paused. With a humorless laugh, she told John Dancer. 'He'll have to swear to the banker that he recognizes me as the true wife and heir of Aaron Blythe . . . '

She broke down again briefly before straightening her small shoulders and adding with understandable bitterness: 'These laws! They won't let a person live in peace, or die in peace.'

'Do you want me to stay with you?' Dancer asked.

'Only if Bingham isn't here. I trust the marshal to keep me safe until the will has been notarized and filed.'

Marshal Bingham was in his office, they discovered, after stepping up onto the sagging gray wood of the plankwalk and in through the open door of the jail. He was a beefy, florid man in shirtsleeves who rose from behind his desk, warm in his welcome of Cassie, frowning at the sight of the tall man accompanying her. After a few words of welcome, Bingham sat again, his eyes fixed on Dancer as if John were a man he had encountered somewhere, at some time, but was unable at the moment to draw up from his memory.

Cassie, invited to sit opposite the marshal, placed her reticule on the desk. Her yellow straw hat she kept pinned to her hair. This was a day to conduct business, and she was determined to appear businesslike. Before taking the offered seat, she drew John Dancer briefly aside and told him: 'I don't know how long this will take. If you could water my horse and wait somewhere . . . ?'

'Of course.'

'You might want to buy yourself a beer in the saloon,' Cassie said. 'I can let you have . . . ' she started to retrieve her purse, but Dancer stopped her.

'I've got some change in my jeans, Mrs Blythe. Take care of your affairs. I'll be waiting somewhere nearby when you're ready to return to the Rafter B.'

The temperature outside was climbing steadily. Dancer paused to remove his hat, wipe his shirt cuff across his perspiring forehead before gathering Washoe's reins and leading the gray up the street toward the nearest saloon where it would at least be shady and the beer, if not cold, would be wet.

There was a sullen atmosphere about the place when Dancer stepped in through the batwing doors of the nameless saloon. It was as silent as a tomb with a dozen or so men in range clothes scattered about, drinking silently as if they found nothing amusing in their desert world. A desultory three-handed game of poker was being dealt at one of the round tables set beside a corner window. The dealer glanced up as Dancer entered, showed no interest and resumed dealing the greasy cards.

At the barrel-top bar itself stood three men in a row, obviously more interested in Dancer's arrival. The man at the furthest end of the puncheon bar wore a flowered-silk vest beneath a town-suit coat. He had cold dark eyes, a strong profile, a narrow nose set off by a thin, neatly trimmed mustache. His companions glanced up in unison as John sauntered toward the bar and ordered a beer. One of these was a fat man with sunken eyes penned in by flesh. He wore an old twill suit, perhaps in imitation of his better-dressed friend.

The third man was a gunhand. There was no doubt in John Dancer's mind what the profession of the tall, whiskered, bitter-looking man was. He wore shabby clothes, but his gun was worn low, meticulously cared for. His eyes observed without being obvious. All three of these had a patent interest in Dancer.

The bartender was narrow, short, an oddly Oriental cast to his features. He served Dancer a mug of beer which proved to be green, tepid, sawdusty tasting, and then backed away into a storeroom behind the bar.

After a muttered exchange of words between the three men at the other end of the bar, the taller, roughly dressed man eased toward John Dancer, his beer mug — Dancer noticed — held in his left hand while his holster rode on his right leg.

'I don't know you,' the stranger said in that way that passes for inquisitiveness, but is also an indirect challenge in isolated communities — especially if there is trouble in the air.

'No, I guess you don't,' Dancer said, half-turning his back to the bar. He smiled at the stranger but it was not an especially friendly expression.

'What's your name?' the gunman asked in a carefully chosen tone. Across his shoulder, Dancer could see the two men wearing town suits watch as their dog growled at the newcomer in their neighborhood.

'You can call me John,' Dancer said quietly. He sipped at his beer and then placed the mug firmly aside.

'I'm Wes Carroll. Heard of me?'

'No. I don't get up this way much,' Dancer answered.

'Mind if I ask you why you're here now?' Wes Carroll asked.

'No,' Dancer said without embellishment.

The gunman began to show a little irritation. He placed his own mug on the counter. 'You haven't got an answer for me?'

'Not one you'd like, nor one I feel in a mood to share.'

Wes began to study his man more closely, and Dancer saw a flash of indecision float through his eyes. Wes, apparently, was the bulldog in this town and he didn't like stray curs. Yet he was wondering if his initial assessment of this strange mongrel's unwillingness to bite had been wrong. There was silent goading from the two men behind Wes Carroll; his owners urging him on to a dogfight, and so Wes continued:

'This is Pinetree range, Pinetree's town. You smell like Rafter B to me. Somebody bring you up here to do a job, maybe?'

'Nobody brings me anywhere,' Dancer said carefully. 'But I am here. Leave it at that.' Wes Carroll's eyes had changed expression again. He stood hunched forward a yard from John Dancer, indecisive and suddenly cautious. He had run off many would-be ranch hands who had come looking for work on the Rafter B. There was something different about this one. He could feel LaFrance and Luke Garner goading him on silently, knew that his reputation and employment depended on how he handled these small matters for his Pinetree bosses, but he suddenly had no liking for the way his opponent was studying him, watching his hands and eyes, his own hand now lazily resting near that polished holster with its cut-out.

John . . . Wes Carroll's mind rushed through his catalogued memories. There were a thousand men named John in Nevada. He could be anyone. But the cold blue eyes of the stranger indicated that he was someone special, someone Wes *should* know.

Dancer shot wildly through Wes Carroll's mind, and at the same moment, in near-panic he scrambled to draw his Colt against the Alamogordo gunman.

He was far too slow. Despite his bluster, Wes Carroll, a big frog in a small pond, had never faced off against a skilled duelist. In slow motion, it seemed, he felt his gunhand drop clumsily to his holster, paw at the Colt riding there. At the same time he saw, from the corner of his eye, men scattering, tables overturning, poker chips scattering across the plank floor of the saloon. That and the oil-smooth draw of the curly-haired man in front of him, the twitch of the wrist which brought John Dancer's Peacemaker up into firing position, the thumb only seeming to graze across the hammer of the big blue-steel revolver as Dancer cocked his single-action Colt and fired.

There was the double roar of the two pistols — Wes Carroll's discharging into the floor, Dancer's sending a spinning lead projectile into Carroll's heart, stopping it. Wes was only briefly aware of the futility of it all, entering a gunfight to please his masters for a few dollars. Then he was no longer aware of anything at all as he pitched face forward onto the barroom floor.

'Murder!' someone yelled. It was LaFrance, the man in the fancy vest. 'Get the marshal! Murder's been done here.'

The fat man with him, Luke Garner, had eased out of the line of fire and seemed content to stay hidden. 'You all saw it!' LaFrance continued, waving his arms wildly. In the corner the poker-players were setting up their table again, scraping strewn chips and cards from the floor. Solitary drinkers at other tables tugged their hats lower and stared into their whiskey glasses.

LaFrance said loudly, 'I'll see justice done!' There was dead silence in the bar room; only the slap of cards whispering through the low, dark room. It seemed that Wes Carroll had been mistaken. This was not entirely Pinetree range, not its private town.

Wes Carroll lay slumped on the floor

like a bloody rag doll. John Dancer backed away from the scene carefully, not knowing what mood might strike the saloon patrons. His hat was tilted back, his Colt leveled in the direction of LaFrance and Garner. Dancer had decided that he did not much care for Nevada.

In a moment he came to like it less.

The mustached man with the Winchester in his hands shouldered his way into the barroom and said with authority:

'You can drop that gun, stranger, or die where you stand!'

4

Dancer carefully placed his revolver down on the scarred surface of the barrel-top bar and raised his hands. The man with the snappy vest, Victor LaFrance, was the first to speak.

'He gunned down Wes Carroll, Marshal. For no reason at all!'

'I saw it,' the porcine Luke Garner chipped in. 'Everyone here saw it. It was plain murder.'

'You're lying!' the feminine voice said sharply. 'You two can't help but lie, can you?' Cassandra Blythe had removed her yellow straw hat and now she waved it at LaFrance and Garner menacingly. 'Walt,' she said to Marshal Bingham, taking the fabric of his shirt in her fingers, 'the only reason there's been trouble here is that John has hired on with the Rafter B. Those two will kill anyone who gets in their way! You know that. Yes, Mr LaFrance, I do know that you killed my husband — I can't prove it, but it's true! I'm a widow alone in a rough country because of you and Luke Garner.'

'Now wait a minute,' LaFrance said roughly. 'I won't be accused like this!'

But John Dancer could see that the woman's words had altered the indifferent mood of the saloon patrons. A scrawny man with pale eyes said from the poker-table, 'I saw it all, Marshal Bingham. It was . . . a fair fight. Wes bit off more than he could chew.'

The bartender, forearms crossed on the counter looked up and told the marshal, 'That's true, Walt. Wes Carroll challenged the stranger and drew first.'

Bingham slowly lowered his rifle and nodded severely, his eyes fixing on LaFrance and Garner. He said, 'You two think you have a lot of leverage in this county, but you haven't near as much as you think. Here's another point to ponder — there'll be a grand jury looking into the death of Aaron

Blythe. You're on notice.'

Then, with Cassie still loosely attached to his arm, Bingham spun on his boot heel and walked toward the exit. Dancer was scowling as he slid his Colt from the counter and holstered it. LaFrance offered him a bit of unwanted advice:

'You're making a mistake, tall man. You've walked into trouble you don't understand.'

'It wouldn't be the first time,' Dancer said, unable to keep the disdain out of his voice.

The bartender was already calling for a clean-up crew and someone to fetch the undertaker when Dancer pushed out through the batwing doors to peer out at the blinding white light off the desert flats. The lingering beer taste in his throat was like bile. A man had died. For no reason at all. John Dancer had lived a brief but violent life, and he had shot men before. That didn't mean he had to like it. He wanted to get . . . away. Just away! If there was any such place as *away*.

Dancer twitched slightly as the door opened behind him on its rusted springs and the shabbily dressed scarecrow of a man with pale eyes stepped out onto the awning-shaded porch. Dancer recognized him from the poker-party and said:

'Thanks for speaking up in there.'

'No thanks necessary. My name's Calvin Hardwick,' the man said, proffering a scrawny hand.

'John,' Dancer replied.

'I had the idea that you were new to the territory and you had found a job . . . ' the narrow man said tentatively.

'I am. And I think I have one at the Rafter B,' John answered.

'Well, sir,' Calvin said, removing his hat to wipe back his stringy gray hair, 'I had heard that the Pinetree ranch was hiring for round-up, and so I wandered up this way out of Arizona.' He laughed drily. 'It doesn't seem now that I stand a chance in hell of getting hired over there. I was wondering,' he continued slowly, 'if you could maybe put in a word for me at the Rafter B. I dearly need work of some kind.'

'I don't run the place,' Dancer had to tell him. 'The line bosses are Charley Spikes and Jared Fine . . . and of course the owner. You just saw her,' he said, nodding toward the bank building where Cassie and the marshal had gone. 'I don't know if they'll be needing anyone or not. I just arrived yesterday myself.'

'But if they do . . . ' Calvin Hardwick asked hopefully. 'You'll put in a word for me, won't you?'

Dancer said, 'I'm not sure my word counts for much, Calvin — but sure, I'll ask the boss.'

The day was so bright it seemed to have gone white. To worsen matters a hot wind had begun to rise in the west, picking up sand and light debris, strewing it across the streets of Potrero. Dancer glanced grimly at the skies; he had seen full-blown sandstorms down on the Texas plains, some so intense that cattle and horses alike smothered. There was a reason for all knowledgeable cowhands wearing bandannas.

The temperature was up into three figures and it was only noon. Pasting himself to the ribbon of shade beneath an awning, Dancer waited for Cassie to reappear from the bank. When she did emerge she seemed no happier or reassured than when she had entered. Behind her Marshal Bingham stood, rifle still in his hands. He touched the brim of his hat to Cassie and said a few indistinguishable words before he sauntered away, giving Dancer the heavy eye.

'Everything all right?' John asked as he escorted the young lady back to her surrey through the fitful sandstorm.

'Oh, the banker says it is,' Cassie said with weariness, 'but one worries. There may be complications.' She offered no more explanation, and Dancer figured it was not his business to inquire further.

Helping her up onto the seat of the

surrey, Dancer noticed Calvin Hardwick standing by, his face mournful and as hopeful as a stray hound. 'Who is that?' asked Cassie, who had also seen the scarecrow man.

'Just a man needing work,' Dancer said, swinging up into Washoe's saddle.

'We have no money to take anyone on,' Cassie answered. 'Not until — unless — we can drive the herd to Carson City.'

'I think he'd be pleased to take only room and board, Cassie. He has nowhere to go. And,' Dancer told her, 'he was the first one to speak up and get me out of trouble with the law back there.'

Cassie was exhausted; that was obvious. The day was hot; the wind was fitful and swirling, tipping and folding the brim of her yellow straw hat. 'I already have Foley on as yard help,' she said with weariness. 'I can't see this man as being much range help.'

Dancer considered this. The lady was correct, of course, but Calvin Hardwick had saved him from — at the least — being locked up on this stormy morning. At last he offered:

'Would you consider taking him on at half-pay, Cassie? The other half to come out of my wages?'

'You know him that well?' she asked with sharp interest. Dancer shook his head uncertainly.

'No. Not at all, but I owe him.'

Cassie hesitated before answering. 'All right, then, John. On those terms . . . but let's get home before the dust storm blows us away!' She clamped her hand down on her yellow hat, slapped the red roan with the reins and started off toward the Rafter B's home ranch. Dancer hesitated a moment, grinned and gestured to the sad-eyed Calvin Hardwick.

'Let's go, Cal!' he called. 'Time to hit the trail.'

With some reluctance, Calvin Hardwick stepped into the saddle of his bay horse and turned its head to follow Dancer out of Potrero. Behind them the doors of the saloon had swung open as the two men in town suits emerged to watch the slow procession. There were no smiles on the faces of LaFrance and Luke Garner.

Dancer gave them little more thought. His main task still was to protect Cassie from any danger along the trail. He briefly told Hardwick what he wanted and sent the somber rider out to watch their left while he rode to the right, still within speaking distance of the widow. After a few miles it became apparent that Cassandra did not feel the urge for conversation that she had shown earlier. Her thoughts were deeply concealed. Dancer could imagine what they must have been, however. What if the Pinetree riders struck at her herd, or worse, at her house? How would she manage the Rafter B with her husband now gone? And, as many a person before her, as she studied the long white land — was any of it really worth it on range that was likely to dry up and blow away? For the Nevada desert was

71

a monument to lost ambitions and broken dreams.

There were three men in the yard when they eventually reached Rafter B. Two of them Dancer did not know. They were both young hands, of the narrow-built sort common on the range. The third was Jared Fine. The big-shouldered foreman's eyes watched their approach with dark interest. The two younger cowboys glanced up briefly and then got back to their work, which was exchanging new mounts for their work-weary cowponies.

Calvin Hardwick held back, sitting his bay horse uneasily as Jared Fine crossed the yard to help Cassie down from the surrey. John Dancer swung down from Washoe to join them. He heard Jared ask: 'How did it go?'

'Everything seems to be all right,' the young blonde lady said, dabbing at her brow with her lace-edged handkerchief. 'I think it . . . '

Dancer could read the concern in her eyes now. Jared glanced at him as if he were a minor annoyance. 'Go on,' the ranch foreman prodded.

'There might have to be a title search done,' Cassie said, spreading her arms in a motion of frustration.

'Title search!' Jared's face darkened, suffused with angry blood. 'The banker told you that?'

'There seems to be some doubt about the water rights, Jared.' She gestured widely, 'About Aaron's claim to all of this land.'

'That's crazy,' Jared Fine said coldly. 'I'll go talk to the banker. I was here when Aaron staked out his land, filed claim to every inch of this territory from here to the Parnassus Hills. I was here, Cassie! It was all done legal and proper. Aaron was no fool.'

'I know he wasn't,' Cassie said. 'I know he wasn't, Jared.'

'Then how in hell . . . '

'There's a conflicting claim.' Cassie now carefully unpinned her yellow straw hat and let the dry wind shift her pale hair across her forehead. She looked exhausted. 'Some mix-up with the titles. I don't know,' she sighed heavily, 'we may have to go to the capital and hire lawyers to set things right. I can't afford that now. Not until we have gathered the herd and driven them to Carson City and sold them . . . if they are our cattle, if this is our water!' she said. Her voice was strong, but it quavered.

'Conflicting claim?' Jared Fine repeated. The big man's eyes were as angry as Dancer had seen them, yet his voice was now under control. 'Someone else filed on this land in those days? Someone who may have a legal right to it? Is that what you mean, Cassie? Who?'

'It can't be that hard to guess,' Cassandra Blythe said with cool precision. 'LaFrance and Garner, of course. And it seems their filing might precede Aaron's.'

With that she had had enough of the conversation, her worries, and the long hot trail. Without another word she walked away toward the relative coolness of the house, her hat held loosely at her side, her eyes distant. Jared turned to glare at Dancer and for a moment John thought the Rafter B foreman was going to wade into him in lieu of a better target for his anger. Instead, Jared only said:

'John, I'm getting more and more happy that we hired you on.' Dancer didn't immediately grasp the meaning of the words, so he only nodded his response. 'Who's that?' Jared asked, indicating Calvin Hardwick who still hung back, sitting his weary bay horse.

'He's with me,' Dancer answered. 'Mrs Blythe said she could find work for him.'

'All right.' Jared studied the scrawny man dubiously; again Dancer expected the burly foreman to find fault, but he did not. Obviously his thoughts were elsewhere. 'Get him to work putting the horse and carriage away and tell Foley we've a new yard man to help him out. You, John, see that your horse is well rested, well fed this evening. Tomorrow,' he added, peering across the river toward the white land beyond, 'I want you ready to ride out with me. I'll show you the lie of the land and introduce you to the line crews.'

★   ★   ★

Evening fell early, the dusk purpling the long empty land. Along the river frogs began to chorus and cicadas added their counterpoint. A long-legged cowboy called Dent had ridden in in time to share their supper, then had fallen immediately into an exhausted sleep. Otherwise the bunkhouse was deserted except for Dancer, Foley and Calvin Hardwick.

At first Foley had displayed resentment toward Calvin, saying he 'didn't need no help' doing what he had been doing perfectly well alone up to that time, but after sundown had darkened the rough bunkhouse's interior and the men had eaten their fill, drunk coffee and cleaned up the dishes, the two older men had settled down into a companionable game of checkers and told each other tales of the old days of which Dancer had no knowledge. He watched them now hunched over the red-and-black game board, chatting with each other like old friends, talking more than concentrating on their checkers, feeling pleased for their sake that he had made the decision to bring Calvin along.

Pleased for their sake, but oddly feeling more alone than he had for a long while, not deeply depressed, but unhappy. A part of that, he knew, was the forced killing of Wes Carroll. He had never wished to return to that sort a life of violence. He had lived it long enough. But there was more to his sadness than that and it was difficult to accept and understand. He watched the two old-timers at their game, sipping coffee and relating old yarns. They had found companionship, someone to talk to and to understand them and their ways. Dancer had never found even such small comfort. Not on the outlaw trail where no man trusted another, not even those he rolled up next to on the ground at night or shared his poor meals with. Such men did not share tales or histories. Their only plans for the future were to survive the next day without being gunned down. Dancer had escaped from that way of life, but he had not escaped its lonely ways.

He filled his tin cup from the half-gallon blue enamel pot on the stove once more and stepped out onto the front porch. The stars were bright, the desert evening still warm and comforting at this hour before the bitter cold of deep night slipped in. From the far desert he heard a coyote howl, echoed in miniature by the excited yipping of three or four pups. The adversarial barn owl he had seen the night before swooped past on broad wings, its shadow cutting a silhouette against the banks of stars in the clear desert sky, on its way to begin its night hunt for voles, fieldmice or any other small creature foolish enough to be abroad. Somewhere nearby its young awaited their owl-breakfast.

The door to the main house opened soundlessly and a wedge of yellow light spread out across the wooden porch and onto the hard-packed earth of the yard. Dancer reflexively backed deeper into the shadows of the bunkhouse awning.

It was Cassie Blythe.

Her pale hair was unpinned, falling nearly to her waist. She wore a rust-red robe which she held around her throat with one hand. Her eyes were searching the eternity between here and never. Her mouth was firm but not bitterly compressed. Dancer had no idea where her thoughts might be, but he imagined that those sad eyes were searching the night for her lost husband, needing his help and comfort in this lonely desert. He remained as motionless as a statue until, after a few minutes, Cassie returned to the house and quietly shut the door, barring it behind her. Then he reentered the bunkhouse, and without another word to the two old men, rolled up in his blankets to sleep.

⋆ ⋆ ⋆

Calvin Hardwick, Foley and the young cowboy, Billy Dent were all up before John Dancer rose from his bunk. They watched him as he wiped the sleep from his eyes, stepped into his jeans and walked along the bunkhouse aisle to join them at the stove where warm cornbread sat and black coffee boiled. Beyond the window the sky was pink with the light of the new dawn. The yard dog barked twice at something and then was silent. In the barn impatient horses whickered for their morning feeding.

'Heard you got Wes Carroll,' the young cowboy with the broken nose said as Dancer drew a chair up to the puncheon table.

'What's that?' Dancer asked sleepily.

Foley placed a tin plate with four squares of buttered cornbread and a cup of morning coffee in front of Dancer and seated himself again.

'Wes Carroll,' the young cowhand repeated eagerly. Dent couldn't have been more than eighteen. Narrow, blue-eyed, a nose that had gotten itself twisted somehow. His shirtsleeves were rolled up as he rested his forearms on the table, hoping for lurid news. Dancer gave Calvin H Hardwick the cold eye. The only way anyone could have yet learned of the bar-room fight was through Calvin. Dancer wanted none of his former notoriety reborn. He said quietly:

'There was some trouble. It got out of hand,' and then proceeded to fill his mouth with hot buttered cornbread, leaving the eager young Dent disappointed.

After eating Dancer planted his hat on his head and made his way toward the stable, squinting into the brilliant sunlight. He found Jared Fine and one of the slender cowboys, a man named Tyrone Terrell, leading their own saddled horses out into the yard.

'I got some business to take care of, John,' Fine told him. 'Get Dent to ride out with you and show you around. He looks like he needs a day off anyway.'

'All right,' Dancer agreed. 'What if we should run across some strays?'

'Hie them back toward the gathered herd if you can, but John,' the big foreman warned, 'make sure whose brand they're wearing. If they happen to be Snake Eye or Double X steers, it's all right to drove them along. Champion and Weaver are going along with us on the drive — those are their brands, but for God's sake, don't push any Pinetree cattle our way. You've seen that brand?'

'I saw it on a couple of their horses, unless they're wearing a different trail brand.'

'No, the rest of us are slapping on a trail brand, but Pinetree will be wearing that five-twig mark.'

Dancer reassured the foreman that he understood him, then stepped aside as Jared and Tyrell swung aboard their horses and trailed out. Dent was just arriving, still munching on a slab of cornbread. Dancer repeated what Jared Fine had told him. The young cowhand nodded.

'That suits me fine. I feel ready to drop after a week of hard and fast roping.'

Within fifteen minutes they were saddled and mounted themselves, Dent riding a little spotted pony that was quick on its feet, built like a cutting horse. On the porch of the big house Dancer caught a glimpse of Cassandra Blythe wearing a blue dress and white apron, hands on her hips, watching them go.

'She's a fine lady,' Billy Dent said appreciatively.

'She's got spunk.'

'Oh, yeah,' Dent said with a crooked smile, 'she's got that. And what makes it more remarkable is that she wasn't born in the West. Aaron Blythe met her back East somewhere when he was on a cattle-buying trip. He left a bachelor and came back with that tiny little bride. People were taking bets on how long she'd last out here, not being used to the long land and the dry winds, the stink of a cattle ranch. But she settled in to learn the business. She took over the books for Aaron, who wasn't much of a man with numbers, even used to ride out on the range with him once in a while on a head count.

'Everyone was wrong about Cassandra Blythe. She's got twice the will of most men in this country.'

Dancer had been listening without hearing, his eyes searching the land which here began to lift and fold into gently rolling hills where purple sage and nopal cactus flourished. Beyond these he could see the sawtooth mountains rising high and stark against the pale sky. There were gathering clouds in the notches, coalescing into a dark mass. John Dancer pointed them out, but Dent shrugged in response and told him:

'The clouds bulge up this time of year, but we almost never get rain from them.'

'Where are the cattle gathered?' Dancer asked the young cowboy.

'We'll get over that way soon. There's a valley — some flats actually — called Tortuga in yonder direction.' He raised his arm to point toward the north. 'That's where we're holding the herd. We'll drift over that way. But first, I know that Jared would want me to show you something else,' he said as they crested the slate-gray hill. 'There is where you don't wish to be riding.' Dent removed his hat and wiped his perspiring forehead with the sleeve of the same arm.

They were overlooking a dry wash clotted with willow brush, which was carved crookedly across the desert below them. 'That's Paiute wash,' Dent advised him. 'It's the borderline between Rafter B and Pinetree. Wander across it at your own risk.' He said quite seriously, 'Those boys *will* shoot. Especially now that they've got it in their heads that we're trying to rustle some of their cattle for the trail drive.'

'How'd they ever get that idea?' Dancer wanted to know.

'Who can tell. Cattle do wander. And there's some even on Rafter B who think maybe Champion or Weaver have picked up a few Pinetree strays.'

'Those are the bootstrap ranchers?'

'Yeah. Double X and Snake Eye. They came into the country late and their land is poor. Just small men trying to make a go of it. I don't know — I'm fairly well acquainted with old Ben Champion, I can't see him as a cattle rustler.'

They drifted northward idly, Dent pointing out a clump of wide-spreading oak trees in the distance, where a pond could be found even at this time of year, and a ribbon of a trail leading further into the rocky hills where one of the three line camps was located.

They dipped down through a shallow arroyo and rode up the sandy slope opposite, the horses laboring a little with the soft footing. They were within a few yards of achieving the flats above when the rifles behind them rang out.

5

Dent cried out in pain, threw his hands into the air and tumbled back down the sandy slope. Dancer kneed Washoe roughly and the big gray crested the rim of the wash. The horse had taken only three strides before Dancer, unsheathing his rifle, reined up hard and swung down from the still-running animal.

Washoe ran on in confusion while Dancer eased his way to the rim of the gully on his belly, his Winchester across the crooks of both arms. Three, four shots rang out from across the arroyo, but whoever was shooting was below Dancer; and he offered them no target silhouette and their bullets flew wide and high.

His hat lost, Dancer crept nearer to the edge of the sandy bluff. Looking down he saw what he had feared. The little spotted horse that Dent had been riding had thrashed its way to its feet, and was now scrambling up the slope toward the flats, its reins hanging free, its eyes wild with confusion. Dent lay face down in the sand, a red stain spreading across the back of his white shirt. He wouldn't be getting up again. Dancer's conscience encouraged him to slide down into the wadi to check on Dent, but his mind, studying the inert figure of the cowboy, told him that it was already too late and that trying to reach Dent would only result in two dead men littering the slope.

He diverted his anger toward settling a score. It was hot as hell. Somewhere distant thunder growled low, like the threat in a guard dog's throat, but the air was still. Dancer's face was sheened with perspiration, and he angrily wiped his eyes clear as he settled in behind the iron sights of his Winchester.

There was a low screen of chaparral on the opposite bluff as there was on this side. Chia, sumac, twisted manzanita, but none of it tall enough to conceal an upright man or pony. Knowing that the ambusher must still be where he had been, unless he had bellied away over the cactus and volcanic rock — unlikely — Dancer forced himself to adopt patience as his best weapon.

He settled in uncomfortably, propped up on his elbows, waiting as the day heated and the thunderheads over the mountains began to creep toward them, their grumbling continuous, ominous. Sweat trickled into Dancer's eyes and stained his shirt, front and back. Still there was no movement across the broad land but the low brush swaying in the ruffling breeze. A lone vulture circled high above them, its dark silhouette like a judgment to come.

Dancer shifted slightly from time to time, wondering if he had mistaken his man. Maybe the sniper had managed to crawl away and was now miles distant. He did not think so and so he continued to wait.

An hour had passed, judging by the

shadows, perhaps more, when the bushwhacker rose from cover across the arroyo and unleashed two wild shots in Dancer's direction. Dancer watched the man weave through the brush, saw him catch up a horse which must have been hidden in a small declivity. The hatless horseman heeled his pony roughly, turning it on its hind legs, intent on a mad dash for safety.

The front bead sight of Dancer's rifle seemed to nestle into the V of his rear iron sights and he touched off, instantly levering another cartridge into the chamber of the Winchester. The first shot missed low. Now Dancer elevated the muzzle slightly, compensating for the fall of the bullet over the distance and squeezed off another .44-40 round. This one tagged the ambusher.

The man's arms flew out wildly and his horse shied violently. As Dancer rose to his feet, readying another shot, he saw the sniper slump to one side of the saddle and tumble from his pony's back. His boot slipped through the stirrup iron as he fell and Dancer watched as the spooked horse raced off across the rocky ground, dragging its dead or wounded rider by the foot.

Dancer lowered his rifle slowly. The rising wind shifted his dark hair and tugged at his blue shirt.

He had been here for two short days and had already shot two men. He might as well have stayed in Alamogordo.

He slid down the bank until he reached the still form of Billy Dent, managed to shoulder the young man and waded back up the sandy bluff. Ahead, in the thin shade of a thorny mesquite tree, Dancer saw Washoe standing uneasily, watching the confusing human games. Nearby Dent's spotted pony stood quivering. Its herding instinct had apparently kept it near the well-trained Washoe. The dapple pony's eyes were wide and it shied away each time Dancer approached it, making John's unhappy task difficult. But eventually he was able to drape Dent's body over the saddle, settle the spotted pony somewhat and swing onto Washoe's back.

The day brooded upon itself; the wind began to gust fitfully and, as Dancer swung into leather the first heavy drops of rain began to fall.

The skies grew dark, and lightning struck near at hand twice, followed by the earth-shaking clamor of sudden thunder. Dancer tugged his hat lower and rode on. Mentally sketching the lie of the land, he turned northward — the wind and driving rain at his back — and rode on toward the line camp that Dent had pointed out earlier. It was much nearer than the home ranch.

If he could find it.

The rain slanted down in pitchforks. Small, quick-running rills appeared where none had been before. The gloom of the day increased. The late sun was lost completely, smothered by the roiling storm clouds. Washoe labored on; Dancer rode with his head bowed, still gripping the reins of the following dapple carrying its master to his final resting place.

Dancer was sure he was lost now. Nothing looked the same as it had at a distance and he had never been in this country before. Water dripped from the brim of his hat, ran down his body pasting his shirt to his back and shoulders. Cursing his luck, he rode on.

Not half a mile further on he became aware of another sort of darkness surrounding him. Looking up he saw that he had entered a small oak grove — fifteen or twenty trees at most — and just beyond the stand of trees a dim light burned in the window of a small stone house. He made his way toward it, Washoe's hoofs sloshing now through shallow mud and rainwater. Dancer approached the cabin with caution, for a new thought had presented itself: what if he had completely lost his way and crossed over onto Pinetree range?

He walked Washoe across the muddy yard of the cabin, and as he neared the door he could now see that it was open bare inches, just wide enough for someone to peer out — or wide enough for a gun muzzle. He hailed the house.

'Anybody in there!' There was a brief pause and then a deep voice answered.

'Yeah, we're in here, and you're covered, brother. What's your business?'

'We got ambushed on the trail. I've got Billy Dent with me. Dead.'

Again there was a pause as if consultations were being held. The voice inside inquired:

'Who's dead?'

'Billy Dent.'

'And who the hell are you?'

'Name's John. I'm a new-hire. Jared Fine sent Billy out with me to show me the boundaries and how the land tilts. We got bushwhacked along the way.'

Again, a brief silence, then: 'Swing down carefully, John. Keep your hand away from your sidearm and come up onto the porch.'

Dancer did as he had been instructed. Before he stepped onto the plank porch, however, he took care to loop the reins to Dent's pony around the hitching rail. It wouldn't do to have the skittish horse, spooked by lightning or its own lingering fear, run off into the storm carrying its somber burden.

Dancer stepped onto the wooden porch of the stone house, whipped his hat to remove the rain from it and approached the dimly lighted doorway with his hands at shoulder height. The door was suddenly flung wide, the glare of firelight bright against the gloom of the storm. A man with a shot-gun in his hands appeared there, backing away to a safe distance as he invited: 'Come on in, John, and tell me again what happened and just who in the hell you might be.'

The fire in the low fireplace with the archshaped stone hearth was bright, but the smoke it gave off seemed heavy and drifted in ghostly fashion across the room. Maybe the falling rain was resisting the rising heat with its cold fury.

The interior of the stone house was

only a single room. On one side of it bunks for four men had been placed against the wall, the upper ones hung on angled chains. The other side of the room held a camp stove, a pantry and a narrow closet. A puncheon table, long enough for six men to seat themselves occupied the center of the room, dividing it. The man with the shotgun gestured with his weapon for John to sit down in one of the roughly hewn chairs. Dancer did as he was told. You don't argue with a man with a shotgun.

The chair scraped the wooden floor. John Dancer removed his wet hat and placed it on the table, then folded his arms on its scarred surface. The man with the shotgun seated himself heavily at the head of the table. His lean face might have been amiable enough in normal times, but now he was scowling deeply, his dark eyes uncertain. He wore an untrimmed red mustache that flared out across his cheeks, a long john shirt and twill trousers held up by black suspenders. The crackling flames in the fireplace ghosted his face with shifting shadows. His shotgun remained on the table, the twin muzzles pointed in Dancer's direction.

His right hand was bandaged heavily with stained muslin. Rusty splotches could be seen where blood had leaked through the poor bandage and dried. Dancer nodded at the injured man's hand and asked:

'Dally thumb?'

The wounded man nodded unhappily. It was a not uncommon injury on the range. A cowboy has to rope a steer quick and fast, drawing his pony to a halt while looping a dally knot around the pommel of his saddle. If he's a little too quick, or a little too slow he risks having his thumb pinched off. This explained why the man was alone in the line shack instead of having been out on the range when the storm broke.

'I was going to cauterize it, but I hadn't the nerve,' the cowboy said. 'Which explains why it's still bleeding two days on.' His eyes narrowed slightly. 'None of which is why I'm sitting here talking to you. Tell me again what happened to Billy Dent and who you are.'

Dancer did, as succinctly as possible. The firelit eyes of the wounded man barely left his face throughout the recital. Nor did the muzzles of the shotgun shift as the cowhand watched, his left hand resting near the double-twelve's triggers.

'How do I know you didn't shoot Billy?' the cowboy asked when Dancer was finished.

'I guess you don't,' John said honestly, his gaze as steady as that of his inquisitor.

'Or that you even work for Rafter B? I sure never saw you before.'

'You can't be sure of that either,' Dancer replied. 'But if I was a Pinetree hand, it would be damned funny — me riding up to a Rafter B line shack. No matter who I might be it would be plain crazy for me to lug a dead man along instead of leaving him where I'd killed him.'

'I suppose so,' the man with the red mustache answered with a heavy sigh. 'That don't make any sense. Things have been bad around here, mister. Everyone is jittery. Billy . . . he was a good kid.'

'You knew him well?'

'He was my cousin,' the injured cowboy told him. More thoughtfully he added: 'Well, my sister's husband's cousin. I don't know if that makes him anything to me. I called him 'cousin' anyway. I brought him into this country with me from El Paso last summer . . . ' The cowhand fell into thoughtful silence. The fire found pine-pitch in a log, sparked and crackled with a muffled explosion.

The red-mustached man's eyes were serious now: perhaps he believed he might have been partly responsible for his cousin's death by bringing him to Nevada.

'This is just bad-luck range,' he said

at length. 'Just plain bad-luck range.'

Later, after they had fallen into a sort of wary amiability, Dancer asked about stabling the horses and was told there was a rough lean-to affair behind the house. Going out into the rain which still drove down, Dancer saw to the chore of stabling the horses. He left young Billy Dent to the dark chill of the lean-to as well. There was nothing else to be done, not on this raging and remorseless night.

Later Dancer curled up on one of the lower bunks, watching the gold and crimson of the dying fire through the smoke that continued to shadow the room. He considered his host's dismal assessment of the situation he had landed in and found himself reaching agreement with him. The two days spent on Rafter B had been unrelieved hell. Two men dead at his hand. Caught in the open in a fierce storm, lying now in soaked clothing on a wooden-plank bunk under a single thin blanket. Someone out on the range willing to kill him from ambush. Maybe it was just as the man said:

Just plain bad-luck range.

Dancer remembered Foley's advice on the day he had arrived. He should just climb aboard his horse and slap spurs to it. That, he could not do with honor, since he had hired on to do a job — no matter that the job he had expected had transmuted into some dangerous undertaking that he did not even understand.

Or, rather, he did understand — all too well. The law of the gun had been imposed, and he was expected to be an officer of that law. It was too similar to the circumstances in which he had found himself in New Mexico. There he had been hired for his skill with weapons, then disposed of — nearly outlawed — when the struggle was ended. He had wanted only to work as a cowhand again, to leave his past behind.

Perhaps, he considered morosely, a man carried his past, his destiny with him and nothing could change the course of his life.

Foley had had a point. There were still a few shoestring ranches further north who would need help at round-up time. When the storm broke, he could ride out in that direction once more. No one would ever know or care — he could be easily replaced. It was a solution to be considered.

Restlessly Dancer rolled up in his blanket, his eyes still open, studying the low-burning fire. He could ride on in the morning. True. But he had given his word. And as he closed his eyes against the firelight he had a vivid image of the person he had given his promise to. A small, golden-haired, widowed woman, her eyes fixed sadly on the past, and so hopefully on her future.

* * *

Chapin — for that was the red-mustached man's name — was up before dawn. By the time Dancer rolled

103

out, the morning had arrived with bright new promise. The door to the stone cabin stood open. There was coffee on the stove, bubbling and boiling, its rich scent filling the room. Dancer glanced out at the skies; they were clear except for a few vagrant clouds orphaned by the storm flock. The birds were chirruping in the oaks; the thirsty desert was rapidly soaking up the rainfall.

'I'll help you with Billy,' Dancer promised as he seated himself at the table. Chapin placed a tin cup of coffee in front of John and shook his head solemnly.

'I'd rather do it myself. He was family.'

'With your hand as it is — '

'I'd rather do it myself, John,' Chapin said with unexpected sharpness.

While Chapin set grimly about his task, Dancer saddled Washoe, considering his next move. It seemed that his best option was to ride on ahead and catch up with the gathered herd at

Tortuga Flats. There he could report to Fine or Charley Spikes — one of them was bound to be around — and follow any instructions they might have to give him.

Chapin, seated at the table with a cup of coffee between his hands, was in no mood for any further conversation, but Dancer did ask for and receive instructions anew on how to locate the flats.

Therefore, he started out through the bright cheerless morning toward the round-up camp. The sun was bright on the remaining dewdrops, scattering jewels across the buffalo grass. Star-flowers and blue gentian seemed to have sprung up and blossomed overnight with the new moisture. These low-growing flowers carpeted the long land prettily. As Dancer passed he startled a covey of desert quail and they took briefly to flight before hiding themselves away in a brushy thicket.

He could smell the herd before he

could see it, and he could hear it clearly. Half a thousand steers milling and lowing in the near distance. Pleased with the warming sunlight, they nevertheless were uneasy, wishing to be pushed onto fresh graze. The low hills were rocky and mostly barren, but the flats when Dancer reached them, were long-spreading and stained with the green of grass. The herd, moving about restlessly, raised a constant bovine clamor. Horns clicked together like castanets. They resented being held so closely packed together.

Two cowboys circled the herd, holding them in a tight bunch. Three or four dogs could also be seen, biting at the hocks of any rogue steer that tried to make a break for the long desert beyond. A low mesquite-wood fire burned near the herd's head. Three or four cowhands crouched near it, sipping coffee or standing to watch the new morning arrive. Branding-irons were being heated there, ready to slap on a trail brand for the mingled

Rafter B, Champion and Weaver cattle, readying them for their long drive to Carson City where the cattle would shortly become table beef for the miners all along the Comstock Lode from Silver City to Elko — men who had no time to waste raising food for themselves while silver and gold waited to be discovered in the heart of the hills.

Dancer slowed Washoe as they made their way down the rocky slope to the flats proper. Heads lifted around the fire and one man pointed, calling out something unintelligible across the distances. Several of the men rushed to their ponies and swung into their saddles. Two of these had unlimbered their rifles as Dancer approached. He held his free hand high to indicate his lack of hostility and halted Washoe. His gesture apparently did nothing to cool tempers. Rather, other men rushed to join them, whooping and yelling to each other and the band of men raced toward Dancer in an angry flood. At their head rode Charley Spikes, and before asking any questions the bearded man, at the gallop, raised the butt of his rifle to his shoulder and triggered off a near shot.

6

Dancer kicked free of his stirrups. Astonished, angered at this turn of events he rolled to the rocky ground, bruising his shoulder and knee. He drew his Colt, knowing that he had no chance against the half-dozen men riding down on him. But why were they! There was no second shot from the ranks of the cowboys. Perhaps they believed that the single shot from Charley Spikes's repeater had found its mark.

Before the horsemen had reached him, Dancer had risen to one knee and with his hair hanging in his eyes he leveled his Colt in their direction. He did not wish to shoot another man, but neither did he wish to be ridden over and gunned down by the boiling mass of riders. Above the storm of sound produced by the onrushing hoofs, the whoops of the cowhands, an authoritative voice boomed out.

'Hold up there! What in hell are you doing, Charley! Hold up, men!'

Dancer glanced over his shoulder to see a rider arriving from the opposite direction. It was Jared Fine, sitting a lathered black stallion. He must have been riding hard after the first shot exploded in the silence of the bright morning. Dancer rose unsteadily to his feet as the oncoming riders slowed their mounts and began to mill and circle. He lowered his Colt to his side, easing the hammer down. Jared Fine was still furious with Charley Spikes, still blustering as he tried to shout at Spikes and calm his stallion at the same time.

'Are you out of your mind, Charley! You know this man,' he said inclining his head toward Dancer who stood unsteadily beside Washoe.

'Yeah, I know him now,' the bearded man replied in surly agreement. He shoved his rifle into its scabbard roughly and complained, 'How the hell was I to know who he was a mile off? He was riding in from the direction of Pinetree. We got no men over in that direction.'

'You know my horse,' Dancer said, forcing himself to still his anger. He picked up his hat and replaced it. 'You've seen it plenty of times.'

'Country's full of gray horses,' Spikes shot back defensively; that was a feeble excuse, Dancer knew. A Western man doesn't mistake one horse for another, nor the way a man sits his saddle.

'Besides,' Spikes went on, 'the sun's still low. We couldn't see nothin' but a lone rider coming in where none should have been.'

Jared Fine was still furious, but a second thought crossed his mind and he asked Dancer, 'John, why are you alone? What's happened to Billy Dent?'

The cowhands, at a rough gesture from Fine, had started to drift back toward the herd to work. Charley Spikes lingered, still looking as if he were the aggrieved victim of circumstances.

Dancer swung aboard Washoe once more, Dancer told the two men about the previous day's shooting, about spending the night in the line camp with Chapin. Jared Fine listened thoughtfully, his anger not subsiding as he learned that another of his men had been killed on the range.

'Pinetree will pay for this,' he muttered when Dancer had finished explaining matter.

'I'll take care of them if you'll let me,' Charley Spikes said with heat.

'I'm not likely to trust your judgement for a while, Charley,' Fine said with irritation. 'How long have you been running cattle? That shot of yours could have stampeded the herd!'

And killed me, John Dancer thought, but did not say. All right — the cattle were of more importance to Jared Fine than Dancer's life. He thought he could understand that. The herd was a way of life; Dancer a passing cloud. Before another argument could flare up, bad feelings focusing again on him, Dancer asked Fine:

'What do you want me to do today?'

Fine pondered heavily on the question, his mouth drawn down, his brow furrowed. He glanced at Spikes — still angry and defensive — and told Dancer:

'Head on back to the home ranch. We've got all the men we need out here right now.'

Dancer nodded to the big man, knowing that Jared was simply trying to separate him and the bad-tempered Charley Spikes. Perhaps later the two would sit down with Cassandra Blythe and decide among them that Dancer was just too much of a problem to have around and cut him loose. If so, John reflected philosophically, it wouldn't be the first job he had lost.

What bothered him more, he thought as he started Washoe southward, was Spikes's animosity, the bearded man's sudden violent reaction to his arrival at the gather. Washoe with that white splash on his chest, the two white stockings on his front legs, was easily identifiable even at a distance. Also, the sun had not been that low, not low enough to blind a man, Dancer knew. He had been riding down a hillslope as he approached the camp, in shadow.

Beyond all that, what would prompt a man — even if he suspected a lone rider to be from the opposite camp — to simply start shooting, having no idea of the man's intentions?

Something was definitely wrong on the Rafter B — the bad-luck ranch. He wondered whether Spikes's motive had been to keep him from seeing what was going on in the camp itself. They were now busy burning a trail brand on the gathered cattle before they were driven to market: the Rafter B's herd, Ben Champion's Snake Eye steers whose brand was simply a dot inside a square and Weaver's Double X herd.

What if there were other cattle being illegally burned with the same trail brand? What if there were indeed Pinetree steers mixed in with the herd and that, in fact, the complaints of LaFrance and Luke Garner were true — that there was rustling going on by Rafter B men? Or by Champion or Weaver? Those shoestring ranchers had little enough and might hunger for more, given the opportunity to grab it.

Dancer wished that it were possible to speak privately, honestly, with the Pinetree owners, but that was a remote chance after the saloon confrontation that had left Wes Carroll dead.

Lifting his eyes to the sky which was still lightly bannered with sheer clouds, and toward the sawtooth mountains to the west, it occurred to Dancer again that Foley's thinly disguised advice that he just hit the trail and ride out of the valley might have been the best he'd yet received.

But now as Dancer crested the sage-screened hill and saw the small house across the slender river, he cast aside that thought once more. If there was trouble afoot on the Rafter B, if there were thieves among the crew, if there was more murder ahead — there was a young, trusting woman in that house who needed to be protected against the storms of disaster. For any evidence of wrongdoing by Rafter B would weigh against Cassandra even before she had had the chance to present her claims to her land and its water source to a judge in the capital.

And bullets, once they started flying, were not particular about their target.

Grimly, Dancer started down the slope toward the house, his thoughts tangled and melancholy.

The bunkhouse was empty as Dancer dragged in. Foley and Calvin Hardwick must have been out taking care of yard work somewhere. There was a strange horse — a stubby palomino — hitched to the bunkhouse rail, he noted, but no sign of its rider.

Dancer tentatively touched the coffee pot with his fingertips, found that it was still hot and poured himself a cup. He had barely lifted it to his lips when the strange rider appeared, his hair and hands wet. He had obviously been cleaning up at the well. Dark-haired, dark-eyed, he grinned when he saw Dancer. Reaching for a towel to dry his hands he introduced himself.

'Jason Burr,' he said. After shaking hands he rolled down his cuffs and poured himself a cup of coffee.

'John,' Dancer replied.

Burr was no more than twenty, but his skin was already leathery from the Western sun. His smile seemed genuine, his good humor congenial. He perched on a bunk and told Dancer: 'I'm glad to meet you.' He spread his hands. 'I'm glad to meet anyone! I rode in at seven this morning, got hired by the boss lady, and haven't seen another soul since.'

'Most everyone is out at the round-up,' Dancer said. He leaned back against the table and sipped carefully at the hot coffee. Why had Cassie hired this enthusiastic young man? Hadn't he been told that very morning that they already had all the men they needed out on the Tortuga? Maybe Cassie figured that on a trail drive an extra hand could be useful, especially with matters standing as they did.

'Where you up from?' Dancer asked.

'Laredo is the last place I had any sort of situation,' Burr said, meaning that he had been drifting. 'How's things around here?'

'There's been trouble,' Dancer told him honestly.

Burr said meditatively, 'Well, there's trouble wherever a man goes, I guess.'

'So it seems,' Dancer agreed darkly. 'Did the boss tell you what we're supposed to do today?'

'I've no idea,' Jason Burr said with a wide smile. 'Truth be told, I don't care much as long as she hired me on.'

It was then that Foley came into the bunkhouse, his arms bare and muddy from some task. He was briefly introduced to Jason Burr; then he told them: 'Boss wants the two of you mounted and ready to ride within the hour.'

'Ready to ride where?' John Dancer inquired. Foley's narrow face was drawn down; his eyes met Dancer's unhappily.

'You wouldn't believe it, but she means to cross to Pinetree and have a talk with LaFrance and Garner.'

None of this meant anything to young Jason Burr, but to Dancer it was a shock. 'Pinetree?' he said disbelievingly.

'That's what the lady said,' Foley replied heavily. 'I'm glad you've come back, John. She was going to go over there with just the kid here. She saw your horse out front and told me to give the message to both of you.' The old man sighed and said: 'Well, now I have to get back to my chores. Take care of her, John! I don't know what she's thinking, but you know Mrs Blythe. Once her mind is made up about something, nothing will stop her from doing it.'

After Foley left, leaving the door open to the bright morning, Jason asked Dancer what the significance of the old man's speech was. Briefly Dancer sketched the troubles on the range between the contending ranchers, not omitting the three killings that had occurred since he had arrived. Jason shook his head more with wonder than concern and Dancer figured that the kid, despite his youth, had already been in a few scrapes in his time.

'I've got to switch horses, Jason,' Dancer said. 'My gray has been traveling a lot.'

'All right,' Burr answered agreeably. 'My palomino's fresh. We made night camp not three miles from here last night. Anything I should do while you're tacking up another mount?'

'Yes,' John Dancer replied soberly, 'check the loads in your guns.'

John Dancer found Calvin Hardwick nailing down a few loose slats on the grain shed. He told him what he needed: 'I've got to ride out again,

Calvin. Washoe's pretty beat up. Do you mind if I take your bay?'

'John,' the scrawny old-timer said around a mouthful of nails, 'anything I have is yours. If it hadn't been for you I'd have no grub today, no cot to sleep on tonight.'

Dancer thanked the man, returned Washoe to the stable, forked hay for the animal and began saddling the bay horse, which eyed him with some uncertainty. Before Dancer had given the cinch one last tug, Jason Burr had appeared in the open double-wide doors to the barn and announced:

'The boss lady's ready ... and impatient.'

'One minute — this old horse is being cantankerous, holding air.' Dancer gave the bay's stomach a nudge with his knee to give the animal the idea that it was time to quit playing pranks, tightened the webbed cinch and, after adding his rifle scabbard to his accoutrements, led the balky bay out into the still-new morning, seeing the sun slant through the oak trees and glint off the face of the river. Cassandra Blythe sat on the bench seat of her surrey, her hands knotted together, her face taut with worry. She brightened as Dancer approached.

'I'm so glad you're back, John,' she told him, and he could hear the relief in her voice. 'I expected you here last night. When you didn't show up, I sort of panicked.'

'Is that why you hired Jason Burr?' Dancer asked, resting his boot on the step of the surrey.

'Is that his name . . . ? Yes. I'd made up my mind to go over to Pinetree and see if we can't work this out amicably. Somehow. Everyone is out at the round-up. Was I to take Foley or . . . ?'

'Calvin,' Dancer provided.

'Yes, Calvin. Oh, I don't really think Victor LaFrance or Garner would harm me, but this is certainly no time for a woman to be riding out alone with all that's been going on.'

Burr was arriving now, leading his

young palomino, smiling as always, yet looking a little doubtful. Dancer said to Cassie: 'Maybe I should drive the surrey. We still have some talking to do.'

'Oh?' Her cornflower-blue eyes opened wider, surprised at his suggestion. 'What's happened?'

'Word hasn't got back here yet — about Billy Dent?'

'What about Billy?' she asked, suddenly anxious.

'That's one of the things we have to talk about,' Dancer told her.

'Very well,' Cassie said, looking even more worried now, as if she were on the brink of a breakdown. Nevertheless, she was determined. As Foley had remarked: once her mind was made up about something, she would do it. Dancer had to admire that in the woman, although the wisdom of riding onto Pinetree range was debatable.

Dancer explained briefly to Jason Burr that the younger man was to be the outrider now. He then tied the lead to Calvin Hardwick's bay horse to the rear of the surrey, stepped into the swaying buggy and unwrapped the reins from the brake handle. He started Cassie's coppery roan on toward the property line.

The morning was fine and clear. They startled a group of yellow-breasted meadow-larks from their feeding in passing, and twice a pair of pheasants. Dancer also spotted a four-point mule deer buck on a low ridge, not far distant. It raised its head and watched warily as they passed. The desert creatures had all emerged from their secret places, it seemed, lured forth by the rainfall which had filled formerly dry *tinajas* and which still left a few silver rills running across the barren land.

They dipped low across the sandy wash which Dancer recognized as Paiute Gulch — the Pinetree border-line, and continued on. Burr, rifle across his palomino's withers, scanned the surrounding terrain for any possible threat as he rode.

Dancer told Cassie about the death of Billy Dent, and she nodded sadly, saying: 'This is why it has to stop, John! This pointless conflict. There must be a way to put an end to it. Let them take me to court in Carson City. If I lose my case, so be it. I do not want any more blood on my hands.'

The country around them was richer than Dancer had been led to believe. Instead of sere desert, they now passed over generous patches of blue gramma and buffalo grass, and there were sycamores and liveoak trees, if not in profusion, at least in plentiful stands. It was difficult to see why Pinetree was so obsessed with driving Aaron Blythe and now Cassandra out of the territory. Except that, he reflected, once men have some, they always want *more*. More becoming in time a twisted obsession. What of Snake Eye and Double X, he wondered. Did Ben Champion and Weaver, having less than their neighbors, feel slighted by Fate?

Dancer let the red roan find its way

while he glanced at Cassie. Her tense, lovely face had grown weary and fearful. He did not like to see her that way. He would have done anything to relieve her distress. He tried chatting about other matters.

'They tell me you met your husband back East.'

'Yes. Aaron was on a cattle-buying trip,' Cassie replied, brightening with the diversion. 'In Kansas City. Everyone was still running mostly longhorn cattle out here — dreadful, cantankerous beasts! — and he had gone East to purchase shorthorns. Now, as you've seen, we run mostly Herefords on Rafter B. All the ranchers do. Aaron is responsible for that; he brought them into Nevada in the first place.'

'And brought you,' Dancer said, unable to disguise the hint of fondness in his voice. She seemed to feel his thoughts on some level, for she smiled.

'Yes, well . . . here I am.'

'What did you do before? Before you met Aaron?'

She laughed. 'Well, I had the idea that I was an actress.' Cassie shook her head. 'I suppose I wasn't any good. I don't know. Kansas City is not exactly New York, anyway. I was in the wrong place, acting the wrong roles . . . I don't know, John, that's a difficult business.'

Dancer nodded. He knew little about it, but it was his understanding that acting could chew up a man or a young woman searching for success.

'So,' Cassie said with a touch of weariness, 'here I am.'

'And here we are,' Dancer said, reining in the red roan.

Below them they could see the two-story white house with a quartet of white columns and its green shutters, surrounded by a flourishing stand of cottonwood trees. Pinetree's home ranch house. It was quiet down in the glade; of course the Pinetree hands would also be out on their gather, trying to beat Rafter B and its partners to Carson City. The first herd to arrive would, of course, draw the highest prices.

Quizzically Jason Burr approached the surrey on his easy-gaited palomino and waited, hands crossed on his saddle horn, for instructions.

'What do we do now, Cassie?' Dancer asked.

'We've come too far to turn back now, haven't we?' she replied in a quiet voice. 'Let's meet the enemy face to face.'

7

They hadn't gotten far before the illusion of a deserted home ranch was broken. Emerging from the cottonwood grove were two men armed with Winchesters. Their faces were grim, their eyes malignant as they read the Rafter B brand on the red roan and recognized Cassie for who she was. Dancer's muscles tightened reflexively, but there was no point in drawing a gun; he only hoped that Jason Burr recognized their situation as well.

'What d'you want here, Mrs Blythe?' the bulkier of the two armed men asked. He was pockmarked, slope-shouldered and wary.

'To speak with Mr LaFrance or Luke Garner — whoever is here at the moment,' Cassie said with dignity.

'They're both here,' the big man told her. 'Whether they'd consider talking to you or not is another matter.'

'I suggest you find out,' Cassie answered with a regal touch. Dancer, sitting next to her, could feel her trembling slightly, but she was managing herself well.

The pockmarked man sent his thinner companion off at a run to the house while he continued to glare at the two armed men Cassandra had brought with her. 'You boys might as well shed those guns right now,' he suggested. 'We'll take them from you before you enter that house, anyway.'

A third man had appeared from the shadows. He now leaned idly against a tree, his hat tugged low, a pistol on either hip. Dancer glanced at Cassie, whose chin dipped slightly in response to his unspoken question. There was really no choice about it anyway, so Dancer unbelted his Colt, rolled the belt around his holster and placed it aside on the black leather seat of the surrey. Burr, smiling with some inner amusement, eased his bay next to the carriage, showed the Pinetree man his unbuckled pistol and tossed it into the surrey, handing his rifle over to Dancer who stored it on the floor.

'You can all step down now,' the burly man said, and they did so. They stood together in a row for a long minute, waiting for the messenger to return. No one spoke. The big man kept his steady gaze fixed on them. Dancer and Burr flanked Cassie who was wearing a white dress and white hat with a pheasant feather waving from its band on this morning.

When the runner from the house returned he nodded and reported: 'The boss'll see them.'

Without ceremony they were marched toward the front of the big white house, three armed men traipsing behind. Dancer occupied his time studying the lay-out of the ranch and yard for future reference. Burr whistled between his teeth, irrepressible in his good humor. Cassie appeared more impatient to get on with matters than frightened.

The front door to the big house opened on oiled hinges and a house man, an older, slightly timid gentleman in a frayed-at-the-cuffs suit admitted them. Maybe this employee was another example of the Pinetree trying to maintain some façade of gentility, like the unlikely Luke Garner wearing a town suit and a shirt which chafed his fat neck.

'This way,' the white-haired man said, gesturing, and the three were led across a broad, sparsely furnished living room to Pinetree's inner sanctum. Dancer's eyes remained active, drawing a mental blueprint of the house. You never knew when you might have to return to the enemy camp.

The house man indicated an open white-painted door and slipped away up the corridor with evident relief. Inside the high-ceilinged room they found Victor LaFrance seated behind a mahogany desk with intricate scroll-work, a few papers spread out on the desk top. He was in shirt-sleeves now but still wore the flowered-silk vest he had worn in the saloon upon first meeting Dancer. LaFrance did not rise, manufacture an unfelt greeting, or offer them chairs.

'Well?' was all the man with the narrow mustache said.

'We need to talk,' Cassandra said, taking three steps ahead of her two men. There was something pleading in her tone, something steely. She seemed frightened, but determined. Victor LaFrance made an indefinite gesture with his ringed hand and Dancer heard the muffled sound of boot leather across the polished floor behind him. He spun to find Luke Garner there, a drawn .36 Remington pistol in his hand.

'You murdering bastard!' Garner said to Dancer. 'Wes Carroll was a friend of mine.' He stepped nearer, jabbing the muzzle of his pistol against Dancer's chest. Dancer heard Victor LaFrance say something like ' . . . until this is done with,' but he paid no attention to the words.

Luke Garner was no gunhand and he had made a critical error in his brash challenge of John Dancer. He was far too close to Dancer, near enough so that Dancer was able to clamp his right hand around Garner's wrist and simultaneously grip the barrel of the Remington with his left hand, twisting the pistol up and away from his wrist. The sound of the fat man's forefinger cracking was audible throughout the room.

Garner fell away, holding his broken finger, howling with pain. Dancer paused to see if the man would make another move. When Garner did not attempt one he flung the revolver away into the open mouth of the white-brick fireplace at the side of the room. Jason Burr, who had been temporarily stunned, recovered his constant smile.

'I'll have to remember that one,' he said in a low voice.

Garner continued to complain. There were tears in his eyes. LaFrance looked only vaguely sympathetic as he said,

'Go get Wally or somebody to throw a splint on that, Luke.' To Dancer he said, 'Damn fool should have known he was too close to you.'

'You favor shooting from a distance, do you?' Dancer asked, conjuring up angry images of Billy Dent's needless death. LaFrance either didn't catch the reference or did not care. Belatedly he told Cassie: 'Sit down, Mrs Blythe. Tell me why you have honored me with your presence.'

'This has gone on long enough, Mr LaFrance,' Cassie said, settling into a mahogany chair with a green velvet seat and back. She smoothed her white skirt, hesitated, and went on: 'The killing has to stop! There has to be an end to it all — the shootings, the rustling, the threats.'

Thoughtfully LaFrance nodded, taking a cigar that he never lit from a box on his desk. 'I agree,' he said at length. 'But what are we to do about it — so — so long as your men continue to take my steers? So long as you deny me my lawful rights to the water?' He glanced at John Dancer, 'So long as you continue to import gunhands.'

'And what was Wes Carroll!' Cassandra demanded, temporarily losing her composure.

'Carroll was a mistake,' LaFrance said without emphasis. 'As Luke told you, he and Wes were friends some years ago. My partner recommended him, and,' he added with a shrug, 'the way things were eventuating — shifting toward an all-out range war — I offered no serious objections to taking him on.'

'Was it Carroll who killed my husband!' Cassie asked, her voice tremulous and low. LaFrance seemed genuinely surprised at the question. He placed his cigar aside and leaned forward, arms resting on his desk.

'Aaron Blythe was not harmed by anyone from Pinetree.'

'Then . . . ?'

'If I were you I would look closer to home. Ask Ben Champion or Weaver on the Double X where their riders were on that day.'

'Why would they . . . ?' Cassie asked in confusion.

'Because Aaron Blythe had much, Mrs Blythe, and they have nothing. No one in the territory believed you would stay on and try to run the Rafter B with your husband dead. Then, if you left, that would leave the country wide open, wouldn't it? The vultures were gathering.'

'I don't believe you,' Cassie said, looking at her lap where her upturned hands rested.

'Then don't!' LaFrance said, his words showing heat for the first time. 'All I know is that someone is trying to ruin you. Someone is trying to ruin Pinetree. Think about it, think carefully, Mrs Blythe. You have come accusing the wrong men. I will still fight for the claim I hold on your land, I will still pursue a legal judgment for the water rights which I believe I am justified in seeking . . . ' He rose sharply, his chair scraping the polished oak floor, 'But I am not a scoundrel, a bushwhacker, an oppressor of widows.

'Pinetree will fight if it is provoked — take my word for that — but you are looking in the wrong place for your villains. I am willing to let the courts decide our disputes. I have no need to drive off your herd or resort to midnight raids on your ranch. Good day,' he concluded in dismissal and walked past them into the hallway of the house, disappearing into its depths.

Outside again, Dancer asked Cassie: 'Well? What do you think? Was he telling the truth or protesting too much?'

She smiled faintly at his allusion. 'I think,' she answered, tying the wide blue ribbons that held her bonnet into a bow, 'that it was a fine performance by Victor LaFrance.' Burr glanced at her, not understanding. Dancer explained:

'Mrs Blythe was once an actress.'

'I see,' Jason said quietly. 'I think I

see — you both believe that he's a lying . . . '

Cassie's carriage had been drawn up in front of the stately house, the bay horse and Burr's palomino hitched behind. There were still two riflemen standing nearby in the shade of the cottonwood trees. Dancer retrieved his gun from the bench seat of the surrey. He opened the loading gate, spun the cylinder of his Colt to assure himself that it hadn't been tampered with and belted it on.

There were three new horses at the hitch rail when they left; somehow word must have gotten out that Pinetree might need re-inforcements. Dancer guided the red roan past the shadowed eyes of the guards, only releasing his breath when they were past the cottonwood grove and once again out onto open prairie. Then he drew the surrey up and asked Cassie:

'Will you take the reins now? I'd feel better if I were free to ride the bay and keep an eye out for trouble.'

'All right,' Cassandra said. There was a slightly tremulous tone to her voice as she nodded in reply. Dancer couldn't blame her. Nothing had been accomplished at Pinetree. In fact Luke Garner could only have had his hatred of Rafter B deepened. As he sat nursing his broken finger, he would be sure — eventually — to ponder means of retaliation, if not against Rafter B, certainly against Dancer himself.

Cassandra started the surrey homeward at an even pace, the red roan picking its way nimbly over the broken ground. Jason Burr had drifted his palomino pony near to Dancer and he watched the carriage roll on for a minute before gesturing to John Dancer. Dancer guided the bay horse nearer to the young man questioningly.

'What is it, Jason?' he asked as they rode side by side across the rugged land where still small silver pools of rainwater lay.

'I've got to tell you something, John,' Jason said with his habitual smile in place. There was concern in his dark eyes, however. Both men looked briefly skyward as a red-tailed hawk wheeled past, complaining shrilly.

'Go ahead, Jason.'

'I don't know much about what is going on around here,' Burr said. 'I only got here this morning, as you know . . .'

Dancer prodded the hesitant cowboy. 'What is it, then?'

'About all I know is what you've told me and what I heard in that guy's office,' he said, tilting his head in the general direction of the Pinetree ranch. 'But you saw those new horses as we were riding out, didn't you?'

'Yes, I did,' Dancer answered, guiding his pony around a thicket of paddle-bladed nopal cactus.

'Did you notice the brand on that tall Appaloosa?'

'No, I didn't pick that up.'

'It was Snake Eye. A dot in a square, right? I just thought you'd want to know. Me, I'm wondering why a Snake

Eye horse would be on Pinetree range.'

Dancer nodded his thanks and they separated by mutual consent, Jason Burr riding a little way off to the north, Dancer to the south to keep an eye out for any incoming riders. It was curious, that was for sure. Why would one of Ben Champion's Snake Eye riders be in cahoots with Pinetree? Or was the tall Appaloosa Champion's own horse? He would have to ask Jared Fine or Foley what sort of horse the Snake Eye owner rode.

All that was certain was that another storm was gathering over the range. A different sort of storm, a more menacing one which, if not throttled through force of arms, was certain to sweep Cassie Blythe from her land as the wolves moved in.

Thinking it over, Dancer could only come to one conclusion. LaFrance and Garner were already challenging Rafter B's rights to the land and the water supply which fed it. Champion and Weaver of the Double X had only scraggly, dry-country herds, worth little even in beef-starved Carson City. If, however, Pinetree was able to win the water rights and in an agreement with Snake Eye and Double X offer to share water and, say, ten to twenty per cent of the Rutter B's property for each — when and if Cassie was driven away and the land could be divided among them — all three would prosper.

There was so much Dancer did not know, could not be expected to know after only a few days in this country. For example he did not know the sort of men Weaver and Champion were, although Billy Dent had told him that he did not think Ben Champion was the sort of man to go in for rustling.

All right then, what about Champion's foreman or someone else with his own plan for obtaining land and water? It was all dizzying to think of. Like trying to solve a complicated puzzle when first seen. There was certainly a pattern to it if looked at properly, but Dancer could not fathom it; he wandered mentally through his suspicions, finding no satisfactory solution.

★   ★   ★

Marshal Bingham was waiting for them in the yard of the Rafter B home ranch when they trailed in. The beefy, florid man was tilted back in a wooden chair on the bunkhouse porch, his silver star glinting in the sunlight. He rose heavily to his feet as he espied the incoming riders.

Cassie drew her carriage up on seeing the marshal. Dancer and Jason Burr exchanged an uneasy glance. Dancer whispered:

'Have you got any warrants out on you, Jason?' The young man shook his head with a wide grin.

'Not no more, John. I've paid for all of them.'

'It must be me he wants, then,' Dancer said tightly.

'You?' Burr said in surprise. 'What for?'

'There's a little matter of a murder that might not have been cleared up yet.'

Burr studied Dancer soberly for a moment, shaking his head. 'There's a few things you haven't told me yet.'

Dancer nodded, 'A few.' Then he swung down from the bay pony to walk toward Marshal Bingham who waited for him, his thumb hooked into his gunbelt.

'Don't try anything, John,' he warned.

'I've no intention of it,' Dancer said honestly. 'Someone posted a warrant on me, is that it?'

'That's it,' the heavy-set marshal answered phlegmatically. 'Now shed your gun — carefully — for me.'

Slowly Dancer complied. 'There's half a dozen people who can tell you how the shooting happened — Calvin Hardwick among them. He's right here on the ranch. They all know that Wes Carroll drew first.' Dancer spread his hands. 'You're just wasting your time, Marshal.'

Bingham frowned and shook his head heavily. From an inner pocket he removed a warrant and straightened its triple fold. 'I'm not here to talk about Wes Carroll,' the big man said. 'You're wanted for the murder of Tyrone Terrell.'

'Who?'

'You ought to know him. He worked for Rafter B. You bushwhacked him up along Paiute Gulch. He was found shot and dragged to death by his horse.'

'Terrell!' Dancer exploded. 'Then he's the man who killed Billy Dent up there. I was only fighting back when I picked him off.'

'A witness tells it differently,' Bingham said with authority.

'A witness . . . ' Dancer was beside himself. Cassie Blythe had come nearer to hear the exchange. Jason Burr, judiciously, had backed off from the confrontation, knowing nothing about the event in question. 'The last time I saw Terrell,' Dancer insisted, 'he was riding out with Jared Fine to catch up with the herd at Tortuga Flats. Jared could tell you that I didn't gun down Terrell.'

'I told you that we had a witness,' the marshal said evenly, his eyes meeting Dancer's. 'The witness is Jared Fine.'

Dancer found himself trembling with anger. At the same moment Fine himself emerged from the bunkhouse, rifle in his hands, his heavy jowls dragged down with fierce emotion. Cassandra Blythe had rushed to Dancer, her hat flying free. Now her slender arms went around him and with her face against his chest she pleaded:

'John, tell them that it isn't so! Tell them!'

Jared Fine had taken another step forward, and now the Rafter B foreman spoke to the woman: 'Cassie, I know you like this fellow, trusted him, but what Marshal Bingham says is so. I saw it happen. The truth is that John, here, is John Dancer, a well-known gunman and killer down in New Mexico Territory. He killed Terrell without mercy, and probably Billy Dent as well so that Billy couldn't testify against him after the shooting. We all know that he also killed Wes Carroll. I don't know who Dancer is working for, we can only guess, but it is certain that he committed murder not once, but twice, and probably three times.'

'John . . . ' Cassandra's fingers had been working the fabric of Dancer's blue shirt. Now her hands hesitated and she let them go slack. There was a flood of tears in her eyes as she looked up into his and begged, 'Tell me it isn't so!'

'It isn't,' Dancer said, his eyes firmly fixed on Jared Fine's lying face. 'Terrell — and Jared — ambushed us, killing Billy Dent. I shot Terrell as he was trying to make his escape.'

'Jared!' Cassie said in confusion. The man lied again:

'How long have you known me, Cassie? I came out to this country with your husband and helped build Rafter B. John Dancer is a killer by nature, and he killed Tyrone Terrell. I give you my oath on it. Do you need help with your prisoner, Bingham?'

8

Cassie had a brief, impassioned talk with Marshal Bingham, but the big lawman remained impassive. Dancer heard him say: 'I have my duty to do,' and then the two separated, leaving Cassie to stand alone on the bunkhouse porch, her hands tightly gripped.

The marshal had kept one eye on Jason Burr, his rifle at the ready, but Jason did not make a move. He had no stake in this, Dancer understood and it would have been foolish for him to intervene, not even knowing the truth of matters.

'I'd like to get my own horse, marshal,' Dancer said. 'Hell, someone will likely be prosecuting me for horse-stealing if I ride out on the bay.'

Bingham remained expressionless. 'We can do that. Though you won't be needing your horse again for a while, if ever.'

They crossed the yard, Bingham a few feet behind Dancer, his cocked rifle at the ready. Inside the barn Washoe stood with three other ponies, his ears pricking as he saw John approaching.

'You go ahead and saddle up,' Bingham said.

In the back of the barn, raking up, stood Calvin Hardwick. He studied Dancer with mournful eyes as he smoothed out the blanket on Washoe's back. The old man looked at the marshal who stood to one side of the open door, his rifle held ready for action. 'Is it serious trouble, John?' Calvin asked.

'Nothing for you to worry about,' Dancer said, hefting his saddle onto the big gray's back. 'Just a little misunderstanding.'

Calvin shook his head worriedly, not believing Dancer's reassuring words. John gave Washoe his bit, still under Bingham's steady gaze. The marshal was an old hand at this business and ready for anything. There was no attempt worth making that had any chance of success.

'I'm ready, I suppose,' Dancer told the lawman.

'All right. Lead your pony out in front of me. You don't mount him until I'm in my own saddle, understand?'

Dancer only nodded. Calvin watched in dismal silence as his new and only friend led his horse out into the bright sunlight. The tableau in front of the bunkhouse had not altered appreciably. Jason Burr stood alone, his thumbs hooked into his trouser pockets. Cassie stood in the shade of the porch awning, watching his approach with wide eyes. Jared Fine held himself at a distance from the young widow, his face still dark with anger.

Bingham said, 'Tuesday, Jared, we'll need you at the courthouse to swear to the truth of the complaint.'

'I'll be there,' Fine promised.

'Can . . . anyone visit him?' Cassie asked with subdued anxiety. Bingham shook his head heavily.

'I wouldn't recommend it, Mrs Blythe.' Cassie's eyes met Dancer's once, briefly, and then she turned her face away, holding her kerchief to her eyes. Bingham swung aboard his sorrel horse and instructed John to climb onto Washoe's back.

'You know the way, Dancer,' the lawman said and John nodded, kneeing Washoe into a gently cadenced walk. He was in no hurry to reach the end of this particular trail.

The sky was blue crystal, the sand flats mirror-white. The distant sawtooth range stood out starkly in vision. To the north where the land began to roll and grow vaguely green they could see a plume of dust rising high into the desert air.

'Looks like they're starting the combined herd toward Carson City,' Bingham said, only to fill the silence. 'Kind of late in the day for it, though.' Dancer looked that way and nodded.

'You know I didn't murder Billy Dent or Terrell, don't you?' Dancer asked.

'I know a complaint was filed,' Bingham said heavily. 'When that's been done, I arrest the man who's been accused. The rest is up to judge and jury.'

Dancer nodded, having expected no other sort of reply from the experienced lawman. Bingham, he supposed, had given up making moral judgements years ago. If he did his job exactly as it was defined, no blame could be attached to him.

Dancer was still watching the northern skies. Now he said: 'That herd's moving in the wrong direction.' Bingham squinted into the sunlight, looking that way again.

'Probably the wind's shifting the dust,' he suggested.

Dancer shook his head. 'No. That's the combined herd, all right, but it's moving to the north, not westward.'

Bingham was frowning deeply now. Hesitantly he slowed his sorrel horse and studied the column of shifting dust as it passed slowly across the distant landscape. 'They can't be trailing north. The only road up that way is through a narrow pass in the hills. There's no way they'd choose that route. The trail's too difficult.'

'Unless they are trying to conceal the herd,' Dancer said. Now both men had halted their horses to squint across the distances of the sunbright land.

'It's the long way around to reach Carson City, that's for sure. We must be wrong,' Bingham answered, although now his voice was doubtful.

'It's the best way if they are trying to keep anyone from coming across rustled beef. The way they're going they could have that herd across the county line before the sun goes down. They made sure that you'd be too distracted to look into it, that you'd be too busy taking me in. They figured to be long gone before you could know anything about it, let alone follow.'

'I don't buy that,' Bingham said as his horse shifted its feet uneasily. 'It can't be. Mrs Blythe would never be party to such a thing.'

'It wasn't Mrs Blythe who sent for you, called you out to the ranch to arrest me! Filed the murder complaint!' Dancer was furious, pleading for belief. 'It was Jared Fine, can't you see that? Him, Luke Garner, maybe in cahoots with Snake Eye and Double X.'

'Jared wouldn't do anything like that,' Bingham said. 'Not knowing the position that Mrs Blythe is already in. I know him, Dancer — Jared Fine came out here twelve years ago with Aaron Blythe. He helped open this range.'

'And what has he gotten out of it?' Dancer asked.

'I don't follow you.'

'Don't you? What has Jared Fine gotten for those twelve years of work? Does he have one acre of land, six steers to call his own? House, wife, family? Maybe he was hoping as much as anyone else that Cassandra would just give it up. Maybe he had hopes that she would fall into his arms, needing his protection after Aaron was hung.

Maybe he killed Aaron Blythe himself, for his own reasons.'

'For what reasons?' Bingham asked, showing genuine concern now.

'For what reasons!' Dancer said in exasperation. He waved a hand toward the country beyond. 'For cattle, land, money. For a fine house and a young widow.'

'I don't like your insinuations.'

'I don't like them myself, Bingham! You could at least consider what I'm saying. We could ride north and see whose cattle those are and where they're going. Who exactly is driving them.'

Bingham was long silent. The hot desert air shifted their horses' manes and tails as they looked down from the rocky ridge toward the gray-green flats beyond. At last he shook his head. 'I have to deliver you to Potrero first. I can't take the risk of riding off anywhere with you. They're expecting you at the courthouse, and that's my first duty. I've a warrant on you for murder. I can't be in two places at once. After I've got you booked and jailed, I may have to come back and take a look.'

'It'll be sundown by then! They'll have that herd started toward Carson City, out of this county. Then you can do nothing at all, Bingham!'

'I am responsible . . . ' Bingham began to say, and then he was not responsible for anything at all, never would be again. The rolling echo of a rifle shot rattled across the barren land and Bingham stood straight up in his stirrups, clutching at his heart before he tumbled head first from the saddle to lie sprawled crookedly against the sand and red rock.

John Dancer kicked free of his stirrups and dove for the ground in a roll, hitting it before a second searching shot was fired, ricocheting off rock with a deadly whine.

Not again! was Dancer's first thought. Was the whole country infested with men with rifles waiting to ambush any passing rider? The thought only flickered through his mind. He turned immediately to more practical matters. Crawling ahead on hands and knees, he was able to reach the marshal's inert body and free Bingham's pistol from its holster. What he needed was a long gun, but Bingham's sorrel had danced away from the dead man in panic and was nowhere to be seen.

Directly in front of Dancer was a stand of cholla — jumping cactus — screening him behind their silver-thorned joints from anyone wishing to shoot again. His attacker could, of course, empty his magazine of bullets, hoping for a lucky hit, but that was a foolish tactic to adopt: a waste of ammunition and likely to increase the chance of drawing attention from any passing rider.

Sweat trickled into Dancer's eyes. He scanned the distances, listening intently, but he heard nothing, saw no movement out on the desert. His grip on the revolver was too tight, his hand damp with perspiration. He tried to slow his pulse by taking in and slowly letting out deep breaths. That served little purpose. The sun was on his right shoulder now. Long minutes passed and he seemed to be able to actually see the spiny shadows of the cholla slowly stretch out from beneath the cactus plants. Flies had found him now, found Marshal Bingham and they paraded across the marshal's face as his open eyes watched. Dancer spared a minute, no more, to think about his own mortality.

He could not stay where he was, nor was there cover in which he could lose himself. He decided on a dangerous ploy — one which could get his loyal ally killed as well as himself.

He whistled up Washoe.

The big steel-dust came toward him, his reins dragging, not understanding what was required of him. Dancer looked around once more and then rolled under the horse's belly, rising on the gray's right side, away from the direction from which he had been fired on. Carefully, he collected the reins and walked away, using the big horse as a shield, hoping that the sniper would understand the folly of trying to take the horse down at a distance. If his attacker did open up again, however, a lucky bullet could indeed kill Washoe and leave Dancer fully exposed on open ground.

Fifty feet they made, traveling shoulder to shoulder, and then fifty yards and still no bullets rang out. After a long, incredibly cautious look around the suffering land, Dancer chanced it, swung into leather and heeled the gray into a run. There were no following shots. Dancer slowed Washoe, patting the big horse's neck gratefully, settling it into an easy walk. No matter who was behind him, running Washoe over broken ground under the hotly glaring sun was no option. If Washoe were to founder, he would be in every bit as bad a position as he had been previously.

Dancer saw movement to his right in a shallow, willow-brush-clotted wash and he turned his gun that way. Then, with relief he recognized the bulk of the shadow, realized that he had caught up with Bingham's horse. He guided Washoe that way.

In the gully, where insects swarmed and hummed around his face, Dancer took the rifle sheath from the marshal's saddle and fastened it to Washoe's rig. Then he unsaddled Bingham's horse, slipped its bit and unbuckled the throat latch, slipping the bridle from the sorrel.

'Get out of here now!' he said, slapping the horse's rump, and after a minute's uncertainty the sorrel began to lope off in the direction of Potrero.

As soon as the horse reached town, it was bound to be recognized and reported. In the courthouse they would have knowledge of where Bingham had gone and what his mission for the day was. There would be no posse formed immediately, however. Shopkeepers and businessmen are not eager to lock up and ride out in search of a killer who could be riding in any direction. Besides, he thought, glancing at the sky, it would not be that much longer before an early dusk settled in across the desert, making tracking nearly impossible. They would find Bingham in time — the buzzards would show them the way.

For now John figured he had the time to settle a few matters. He rode steadily northward, toward Tortuga Flats to settle matters with Jared Fine. The miles passed slowly, the sun beat down unmercifully.

The low sun was flushing the mountain slopes with color, dusk was purpling the long sand desert by the time he caught up with the herd. They were following what appeared to be a little-used trail which angled up and into a canyon cleft. Not the route a man would normally choose with a herd that size.

The steers were being pushed at a

steady pace, urged on over the rough trail at a pace the cattle did not like — not this close to the time of evening when they normally bedded down. Apparently Fine was intent on driving the cattle across the county line before dark. Once they had passed that boundary there was no legal way for them to be halted. Likely no one would try.

Unless Pinetree decided to start a full-blown range war and was willing to fight it in the dead of night. Remembering the grim determination of Victor LaFrance and the unpredictable anger of Luke Garner that was not as fanciful as it seemed on the surface.

Let them fight it out, Dancer thought with his own brand of wild anger. He did not care if the ranchers all killed each other, if the cattle were stampeded for a hundred miles in every direction, with everyone's hopes for a huge beef sale scattered to the winds by their own stubborn hatred, jealousy and greed.

Let them fight it out — he was still

riding for the brand, but his mission was to save it from itself. To stop Jared Fine from profiting in any way from his murderous schemes.

It was full dark by the time Dancer did come upon the herd. They were still being pushed north, by the light of the stars and the white glow of the rising half-moon. He could see starlight glinting on the horns of the cattle, see the ranch hands in silhouette, pushing the weary, unwilling steers onward. Dancer halted Washoe for a moment, letting the steel-gray blow. Where among that surge of men and cattle could he find Jared? He paused briefly, his anger stilled enough for him to consider that if he was caught he was certain to be gunned down. The only advantage he did have was the night itself. No cowhand, his mind on his work, cursing and driving 200 balky steers over the broken, narrow trail, was likely to even glance his way, let alone recognize him. No, he did not feel that he would be challenged once he reached the herd.

He frowned slightly now, searching the dark land. Had Jared Fine posted outriders to alert him in case any incoming rider tried to intrude? Men whose only job was to prevent any unwanted men from interfering. It seemed likely, not because Fine would fear Dancer that much, but because somewhere on the desert Pinetree would be riding. Dancer was now sure of that.

Victor LaFrance would not give up so easily. There would be outriders watching for interference.

Where would Jared Fine be, John now had to consider? He wouldn't be riding drag where eating the dust of hundreds of steers made for dismal work. Nor, Dancer concluded, would the Rafter B foreman be at the head of the herd. For one reason: if Pinetree hit the herd there was bound to be shooting, and at the first gunshots the spooked herd would certainly stampede up the narrow canyon. No man with any sense would willingly ride point in circumstances like these.

Dancer realized that he was again engaging in idle speculation which, if not acted upon, was utterly pointless even if his surmises were correct. Washoe had caught his breath by now and he tossed his head anxiously, eager to be on with the night's business whatever it might prove to be. Dancer was less eager, but more determined. Speculation was useless. It was time to act.

He started Washoe down the rocky slope toward the herd.

Reaching the heated mass of lowing, angry beasts, of swearing, shrilly whistling cowhands, Dancer uncoiled his own lariat and merged with the shadowy bunch, flagging a few steers in passing. No one seemed to notice him or care who he was. One older hand who was circling the herd did glance at Dancer curiously, but John decided that it was because he was riding bareheaded. But many a man has lost his hat along the trail, and it wasn't a significant enough sight to cause the cowboy undue curiosity.

A half-moon had been on the rise, but now as the trail climbed deeper into the dark canyon, it was again smothered by the jutting surrounding hills and the shadows grew deeper than ever. Dancer worked his way along the flank of the herd, his eyes searching the riders. It was impossible to see a man's features or even to tell what color horse he was riding in the swirl of dust, the gloom of night.

After fifteen minutes or so, the rising half-moon appeared once again, peering through a notch in the broken hills. Its thin light illuminated the trail as they began an even more rugged ascent. Dancer wondered if the herd's arrival had been planned to coincide with the cresting moon.

Now, here and there, he could make out men he had seen at Tortuga Flats. He could even read the brands on the cattle. The horses took on color as the moon drifted higher. The canyon now closed in upon them even more tightly — a gray, rocky wedge through the massed hills. Dancer found himself growing uncomfortable in the tight limits of the narrow pass.

He looked across the rolling bulk of the cattle's backs to the riders on the opposite flank, then glanced behind him. He stiffened abruptly as the specter appeared, his hand tensing on his rifle.

Out of the shadows came the big black, moon-glossed stallion with Jared Fine on his back. Fine was a distance back still, but he was riding forward with seeming interest as he studied Dancer and Washoe. Then curiosity was replaced by certainty and Jared let out a yell. 'Hold that man!'

One cowhand raced his buckskin horse toward Dancer, trying to grab Washoe's bridle, but John rapped his hand hard with the barrel of his Winchester, cracking bone. The cowboy yowled and withdrew. Fine was still coming, his stallion now lifted into a dead run. Dancer looked around wildly, but there was no way out of the canyon's cramped confines. He had made a mistake in judgement, goaded by his own temper. Now he would have to pay. Dancer waited grimly, watching Jared, followed by two outriders, bear down on him. Fine raised his arm in a wild gesture and one of the cowboys raised his rifle to his shoulder. It was then that the Pinetree riders set upon them.

9

The roar of the guns was like sudden thunder in the narrow canyon. LaFrance, it seemed, had played his last trump card well, for there were riflemen above them in rocky crags, firing down at the Rafter B men. The cattle as one lifted their heads and began to stampede, adding the rumble of their hoofs to the tumultuous night.

Dancer swung Washoe away from the herd just in time to avoid a wide-eyed, onrushing red steer. There was no telling how many men had gone down before the volley of gunfire, how many had been trampled by the surging steers. Surely the men riding point would have had to do some fancy riding to avoid the panicked herd.

Some of Jared's men tried to fire back at the ambushers, but they needed to be more intent on avoiding the onrushing herd on their panicked cowponies than on shooting. Besides, the riflemen on the cliffs offered no distinct targets, there was only the constant flare of their rifle muzzles to aim by. For the most part, Dancer saw, the Rafter B crew was attempting to escape, not on fighting what could only be a losing battle in the stony chute.

A group of three cowboys who seemed to know their way raced past him, flagging their horses with their reins or with hats, urging them on with curses. Dancer heeled Washoe and fell in with them. If there was a way out of the canyon, they were more likely to know it than he. They rode on at a dead run. One of the cowhands had the bad luck to have his pony — a stubby dun with a Snake Eye brand on his hip — lose its footing on the rocky ground, slip and slide backward directly into the chaotic stream of cattle.

No one glanced back to watch him die beneath the pounding hoofs of the rioting herd.

A hundred yards on Dancer saw the riders swing to the right, into a narrow feeder canyon. And he followed them. Fine might have come this way as well, if he had escaped the stampede. If he had been trampled back there, through his own folly, well, Dancer thought without pity, it was poetic justice.

The moon was hidden again as they entered the steeply walled canyon, narrow enough for only a single horse to travel it at once. Their way zigzagged up the face of the canyon wall for perhaps a hundred yards and then widened as they emerged onto a moonlit flat where the scent of sage was heavy and he could see a long stretch of broken ground studded with agave, greasewood and yucca. He could still hear the thundering stampede in the canyon below. By the time they reached the head of the chute, Dancer considered, the cattle would be dead tired, and if there were more Pinetree riders stationed there, they would be able to collect the herd without much resistance and drive them on their way toward Carson City with only a few hundred pounds of beef run off their bones.

It seemed that LaFrance and Luke Garner had won in the end.

Dancer followed the two riders ahead of him at a distance. They were talking between themselves, but he could make out none of their words. Their horses were weary, their own pulses still racing. Perhaps they were discussing finding an easier way to make a living.

As yet they had paid no attention to him at all. Now he reined up, letting Washoe blow again. Scanning the distances he thought he could make out a light from Rafter B's home ranch. Would that be where Fine had gone if he had survived? There was no telling. Maybe the disgraced foreman would simply slink out of the territory to try hatching a new plan in another place.

Once more Dancer was proved wrong.

He heard the onrushing hoofbeats behind him, swung his head around in time to see Jared Fine's black stallion charging across the flats toward him. Fine drew his horse up in a lather, unsheathed his rifle and took careful aim. Dancer dropped to Washoe's side and rolled to the ground. A boulder he had not seen in the darkness was waiting and he fell onto it, smashing ribs. The breath rushed out of him; pain encased his chest. He fumbled for his handgun, could not find it on the dark earth.

Fine fired again.

The sound of the rifle's report racketed across the flats. This bullet too tagged Dancer. It smashed through his ankle, tearing bone into fractured splinters, severing tendons and muscle. It felt as if a blacksmith had laid his foot across his anvil and taken a sledge hammer to it. Dancer again searched for his pistol in the darkness, again failed. Jared Fine was still coming, but slowly. Too slowly. He wanted to be sure of his man, it seemed. But looking that way through the hair that screened his eyes, John saw that his big black stallion was standing dead in its tracks, frothing and trembling. It wasn't patience that had stopped Fine, but a foundering horse which could run on no more although Fine continued to whip it with his quirt.

Dancer needed to get back in the saddle. There was no way Fine could follow — if he could do it. He tried to rise, but his foot gave way. Fire shot through it; broken bone grated. His ribs protested just as violently. He was never going to make it into leather, not in this condition.

Looking under Washoe's belly, Dancer could now see Jared Fine dismounting, starting toward him on foot. Desperation prodded Dancer's next move. He shoved his hand through Washoe's stirrup, and clamped his other one to it, his fingers gripped tightly together.

'Run!' he shouted, and after a

fraction of a moment's hesitation, the well-trained Washoe did as he had been commanded. A rifle shot rang out and another as Fine raced toward him shooting wildly as he ran after them.

Dancer's shoulder slammed against another rock and his body took another jolting blow. On foot Fine would never catch Washoe. He could run after them for a while, but if Dancer could only hold on long enough . . . just hold on.

Washoe raced on through the night, over rocks, through stands of sage and sumac. Dancer heard another rifle shot, but he could tell by the sound of it that it was over a great distance. Jared Fine would be trying now to bring Washoe down, but in the darkness with Washoe gaining distance with every long stride, his chances were slimming. John now thought he had a chance of making it.

So long as he could hold on to the stirrup. Dancer's shoulders seemed half out of their sockets. His chest burned as if enraged rib monsters were tearing it apart. He could no longer feel his foot at all. His vision was blurry; swarms of colored dots swam behind his eyes.

So long as he could hold on. So long as he did not black out with the pain.

So long as . . . and then the demons had their way and he fell into a dark swirling tunnel, longer and darker than the route to Hades.

★　★　★

The room in which he found himself on awakening seemed familiar, but he couldn't remember ever having been there before. The bright sunlight through a half-open door was stunning. He closed his eyes again. Shifting slightly on the hard cot he saw a man in the corner of the room watching him. He, too, seemed somehow familiar, but Dancer could not remember him either. Pain returned as he awakened and he touched tightly bound ribs gingerly. The agony in his ankle was nearly enough to wish himself lost again in the blackness he had been haunting for the last . . . ?

'How long have I been here?' he asked with his eyes still closed.

'This would be your second day, but you ain't staying.'

'Chapin?' Dancer asked, remembering the red-mustached man's name.

'That's right.'

'Then I'm out at the line camp. How did I manage to get here?'

'You'd have to ask your horse. I suppose it remembered the way.'

'Where is Washoe?'

'I put him up out in the lean-to. I wrapped those ribs of yours as well as I could, put some plaster on a few other bumps and nicks you got. The foot,' Chapin said with a shake of his head, 'I didn't even try to touch it, not when I saw the bullet hole going through your boot from side to side.'

'I thank you for what you did,' Dancer said sincerely.

'I wouldn't leave a dog out in the yard in the condition you were in.' Now

Chapin's tone grew more serious. 'But you have to leave now, John. I can't have you here. This job is all I'm likely to ever have from here on out.' He reminded John of his missing thumb by holding up his now cleanly bandaged hand.

'I didn't mean to cause you trouble,' Dancer said. 'As soon as I can. . . . ' he said, trying to sit up as his broken ribs shouted with pain.

'You can leave *now*,' Chapin said with little pity. 'I'll help you to your feet. Then I'll get you into your saddle if I have to throw you up on it. You're trouble, John, too much trouble for me to handle.'

'I've got to get to Mrs Blythe's house,' Dancer said as he sat on the edge of the bunk breathing roughly, holding his side.

'No, you don't,' Chapin said strongly. 'You aren't listening to me, John. I been down there. The word is that you were working with Pinetree all along, that you helped them rustle the big herd on its way to market. Mrs Blythe lost just about every cent she had. Now she'll lose this ranch, barring a miracle.

'Besides, don't you think Jared Fine and Charley Spikes would love to see you?'

'Fine made it?'

'He made it. He's back. They'll have a sharp eye out for you, you can bet on that. Besides, there's a little matter of three or four murders, including Marshal Bingham's, hanging over your head. No, John,' Chapin said severely, 'you are going to let me help you into the saddle and you are going to ride out of this county. If you ever come back they'll either shoot you down like a dog or string you up — that much is certain.'

* * *

That was how John Dancer had eventually happened to ride into Brownsville. Scarred, broken and bitter. He lay awake many a night in his hotel

180

room planning his revenge. He wished he were a forgiving man, but a saint would have had a problem finding forgiveness in his heart for Jared Fine.

The long three days of the ride back to Nevada gave Dancer plenty of time to think over his decision, to consider the wisdom of simply riding on, past the Rafter B and its troubles. Perhaps if it were only his wish for revenge that drove him onward, he would have done that — leaving the bad-luck range behind for ever.

But Cassie was still there. What had become of her life since the night raiders had driven off her herd? Had the court in Carson City supported her claim to the land and to the water rights, or was she totally without resources now, due in no small part to the machinations of Jared Fine? Try as he might, Dancer could not forget her blue eyes, her delicate figure. He had seen her collapsed with grief as she attended to her dead husband, then had seen her draw upon some inner strength, determined to fight on for what was hers only to have the carpet pulled out from under her.

No, Dancer thought now as the long ride was taking its toll on his injured body and the high, white sun scorched his back, he could perhaps have swallowed his fury against Jared Fine and let him have his triumph, but he could not in good conscience leave the young widow to the gathering vultures.

★   ★   ★

The new morning dawned in muted tones. The sawtooth mountains were draped in dark clouds and the wind across the desert flats was rising, drifting sand across the land, spurring an occasional dust devil up to twist across the landscape. Dancer studied the dark morning sky thoughtfully. It had rained only once before this year, that was when he had been riding for Rafter B. Now it looked to be fixing to storm again. Was that some sort of omen, a warning to stay away? The wind folded back the brim of his hat as he sat Washoe, looking out across the land he knew not well, but too intimately. Below him was Rafter B range. He saw no cattle along the banks of the slow-flowing silver river or grazing on the grass of the shallow vales. No smoke rose from the chimneys of the buildings below, but he was still far away and maybe the rising wind was drifting it away as soon as it rose from hearth or stovepipe.

In other times he would have swung down to ease Washoe's burden, but he had been out of the saddle only twice since leaving Brownsville, lowering himself awkwardly to the ground to sleep, dragging himself back into the saddle at daylight. Washoe was in prime condition. Long rested, exercised lightly every morning by the faithful young Toby Waller, he accepted this unusual burden without complaint.

Dancer could walk. But for no more than five or ten minutes at a time. Even then he moved with a hobble and gingerly step. He was a cripple by almost any definition, would remain one for the rest of his life, he now knew.

The sky grew darker yet. A high dark shelving of cloud began to creep out across the flats. In the far distance Dancer saw a bolt of forked lightning briefly illuminate the black sides. Large scattered raindrops began to spatter the dry earth around him. Reaching back, Dancer untied his bedroll and shouldered into his black rain slicker.

He tugged his hat lower and started toward the Rafter B as the rain fell ever more heavily, the lightning drew nearer and the thunder increased in violence. Down the slope he walked Washoe.

A dark angel riding grimly through the dark and violent storm of an unsettled morning.

Through the mesh of silver rain Dancer could see no men about the ranch. The rain might have driven them to cover. Or, he thought, perhaps there were no longer any hands on the Rafter

B. Perhaps it had collapsed that completely.

However, he could smell wood-smoke. Someone was living here, if only Cassie herself. Of course, she could have finally given up the ranch. Perhaps Jared Fine or even Victor LaFrance now occupied the house and was sitting in front of the fire, warming his feet.

Dancer drew Washoe up in the thin shelter of the cottonwood grove, peering through the driving rain at the bunkhouse, barn, the main house. All was familiar, but he seemed to be viewing it in a dream. The slanting rain intensified the illusion. Lightning crackled near at hand and was followed almost immediately by a cannonade of thunder. Dancer could smell sulfur in the air now and the wind had increased, tormenting the cottonwoods, tearing dry branches free in the upper reaches of the trees.

Washoe shuffled his feet uneasily at the near strike. Dancer calmed the animal as well as he could and then heeled the big gray horse forward, moving out from shelter to cross the yard toward the barn. There still seemed to be no one around. If there was, the constant rain would cover his passage somewhat, and there was no reason a man would be standing at the window staring out at the dismal morning except by chance.

Rain was dripping in curtains from the eaves of the barn's peaked roof as Dancer ducked his head and rode Washoe through the open double doors into the inner gloom of the horse-smelling building. There were three horses inside. Only one did John recognize — the bright-eyed little red roan Cassie used to draw her carriage. The carriage itself sat in a far corner. Calvin Hardwick's sturdy little bay pony was not there. He had more than likely been given his walking papers long ago.

There were at least two men at home, then.

And Cassandra Blythe.

186

There were more, as Dancer discovered at that very moment. He had turned Washoe's head back toward the barn doors when a mounted man wearing a yellow slicker appeared there. He could not make out Dancer's features immediately in the depths of the barn's shadows, but then he did and he grabbed for his holstered revolver.

Encumbered by his slicker, Charley Spikes was too slow reacting as he pawed for his belt gun. He hollered out: 'Dancer!' and as the muzzle of Spike's pistol rose in his direction, Dancer shot the man. The report would have been audible even above the raging storm and Dancer heeled Washoe roughly, breaking for the open. Someone rushed from the front door of the house, and at the head of the awning in front of the bunkhouse, another figure in shirtsleeves appeared.

A shot rang out from the man at the house as Dancer appeared in the yard. The second man, the one who had been sheltering in the bunkhouse raised a shotgun and Dancer changed direction. He guided the racing gray horse up onto the bunkhouse porch and galloped its length, Washoe's hoofs clattering against the wooden planks. Before the man with the shotgun could level his weapon, Dancer had ridden him down.

Washoe's shoulder caught the man in full stride, and he was thrown back off the porch, his shotgun flying free onto the muddy yard. Dancer jumped his horse from the porch and spun it on its heels. Charging back across the yard he rode toward the house, not away from it and through the driving rain he could see the heavy features of the man who stood there, Colt revolver in his hand.

Even then Jared Fine could smile nastily, confident of his superiority in all things. He triggered off his .44 twice, missing the charging horseman both times. Dancer one-handed his Winchester, thrust it in Fine's direction like a knight in the lists, and pulled the rifle's trigger, catching Jared Fine full in the chest.

Fine's arms flailed like a man on a high wire trying to retain his balance. Then he simply flopped backward, his Colt flying free. He lay in the driving rain, his eyes staring blankly up at the tumultuous skies.

Dancer circled the house and re-entered the cottonwood grove as the skies continued to rumble and roar. There was no telling how many other guns might be waiting. From behind the screen of steadily falling silver rain, masked by the shadowy trees, he studied the house and yard intently. The man he had trampled over had dragged himself back into the bunkhouse, leaving the shotgun behind. He was fairly certain that it had been Foley. He regretted injuring the whitehaired man who had probably emerged only to fight for the brand, knowing nothing of the circumstances.

Fine had not moved, could not move as he lay face up in the red mud. About Jared Fine's death Dancer could raise no guilt or sympathy. The man was a scheming killer, no less.

Still no one stirred in the house. Fine was gone, Charley Spikes as well. Perhaps there were no more men there to be aroused by the shots. The loss of the herd might have sent those who had survived the canyon raid traveling on.

After that, Cassie would have been left with no money to pay the hands; what was there to keep the cowboys here?

But where was Cassie? He had assumed that she was here because her pony and carriage were stored in the barn. That, he realized, meant nothing. She also could have long since departed, leaving her coveted ranch to Jared Fine. She might have traveled East once more. Or . . . the thought was like a cold stone in Dancer's heart, she might have fallen to a worse fate. There was no way to be sure. He had to reach the house, to find what truth he could. Risking all, he started forward and came face to face with the armed man.

10

'I could have told them to leave you alone,' said Jason Burr. The young wrangler was smiling as always. He was hatless; the rain had plastered his dark hair to his scalp. His pretty little palomino shifted its feet as he drew it to a halt beside Dancer. 'Looks like you finished the job.'

'I'm surprised to find you still here,' Dancer said, studying the easy-going cowboy. Burr just shrugged.

'I'm not surprised to see you back,' Jason said. 'I told them you'd find a way. No one believed me.'

'Is everyone else gone?' Dancer asked. Jason Burr, his hands resting lightly on his pommel nodded. 'But you stayed.'

'Me? Sure, I stayed, John. I had no place else to go. Cassie wanted to play out the string. She wanted to eliminate

Jared and Charley Spikes right away. I told her to just wait a bit and you'd be back to do the job for us. Hell, what's a couple of more murders on your record? It would leave us without any cloud over our heads if we let you take care of matters.'

Dancer felt that stone in his chest return. Now it was slowly sinking into his gut. He watched the mirth in the smiling cowboy's eyes and simultaneously a small wedge of light crept through the heavy gathering of storm clouds, bringing with it a glimmer of knowledge, distasteful and heart-wrenching.

'You didn't just show up here by chance that day, did you, Jason?'

The younger man laughed and shook his head. 'No, John! There was some trouble out here, I knew. Cassie wrote, asking me to come. You happened to show up in the meantime so she decided to use you until I could arrive.'

'Use me?' Dancer asked numbly.

'I didn't think a man of your

experience could get taken in so easily, John. But I guess a woman like Cassie can cause a lot of confusion in a man's mind.' He nodded toward the inert form of Jared Fine. 'Look at poor old Jared there! She had him on the line, convinced that once he got rid of her husband they could share the ranch.'

'So Jared did kill Aaron Blythe.'

'Sure, him and Charley Spikes. Trouble was, Jared had to go as well. Before he could talk. And, he was totally unequipped to take on Pinetree — I guess he proved that in the end,' Jason Burr said with a chuckle.

'You're lying!' Dancer said with manufactured anger. He was angry with himself, mostly, not wanting to believe he had been taken in, used as a pawn. 'I saw Cassie when her husband had just been hung. I heard her sobs, saw her tears . . . '

Burr laughed again, this time with a sort of raw humor. 'John, don't you remember what Cassie was before she came West with Aaron Blythe? An actress! She can cry whenever it suits her. And lie with the best riverboat gambler you ever will run across. I learned that way back when we were together in Kansas City.'

'You were . . . ?'

'We shared a bed. Is that your question? Off and on. One night she came to me and told me she had a real sucker on the line. A dumb hick who had never seen the big city or a pair of woman's legs before. He wanted to marry her and take her West. She was excited, said he had thousands of acres out here.'

'It wasn't 'til she got here that she found out the real situation. The land was dry, there was little graze, little water. And the thick-skulled Aaron Blythe hadn't ever filed properly on any of it. Seems Victor LaFrance and Garner had an older, better claim to everything Blythe thought he owned.

'Cassie said she had been making up to the ranch foreman, trying to plant ideas in his head, but though Jared Fine was a thug, he wasn't much smarter than Aaron had been. She asked me to ride this way and see if I couldn't set things straight. There was good money in her offer and I thought I wouldn't mind living with Cassie again, so I agreed.

'You just happened to show up first and Cassie decided to use you. First thing she did was take you to town and send you over to a saloon only Pinetree men frequent by common consent. She knew that, and knew that LaFrance and Luke Garner had hired on a second-rate gunhand named Wes Charles . . . something like that.'

'Carroll,' Dancer provided. 'Wes Carroll.'

'Yeah, well, you took care of him, I hear, so Cassie decided you would have your uses if she kept smiling and lying, getting teary-eyed when required. The thing was — Jared Fine did not like it at all. He felt he might be losing some leverage. She told me that one day Fine decided to send you and another hand. . . . '

'Billy Dent.'

' . . . Out to look the range over. Jared and another man — Terrell? — rode out first, knowing where you would be riding and they ambushed you. But Terrell was stupid, took out Dent first. Then you got Terrell.

'Then you started to get too nosy for Jared and Cassie both. You rode out to Tortuga Flats. They couldn't have you looking at the brands on those cattle. Spikes decided to take matters into his own hands — he being Jared's right-hand man and always informed as to what was going on.'

'Jared stopped the shooting that morning.'

'Sure, John! How was he supposed to explain to the marshal that they had gunned down one of their own men? And keep Bingham from coming out to Tortuga where he could see the Pinetree brands on the cattle himself after a murder was reported?'

'And Marshal Bingham's death?'

'Jared got him too. It wasn't enough to have you locked up. There was a chance you might get out on bail or talk too much at your trial. Too, Bingham might have decided to look the herd over for whatever reason and spot those Pinetree brands. There was no risk involved for Jared in killing the marshal. You were in Bingham's custody when he was shot. Who else could have done it? That should have been enough to finally send you riding out of the country to save your neck. The last nudge you needed if you hadn't already gotten the message.

'I could have told them it wouldn't work, that you would not run. They kept underestimating their man. I never did, John.'

Dancer's head was swimming. Everything Jason Burr was saying had the ring of truth. It fit all of the confusing facts together too well. The question was, why had Jason come forward now to relate all of this, to in effect, confess? There could be only one answer.

The smiling cowboy meant to kill him.

Jason must have seen the knowledge flicker in Dancer's eyes, for — still smiling — his hand dropped toward his Colt revolver. Burr said:

'I always wondered if I was better than John Dancer, the famous Alamogordo gunman!'

The balky little palomino side-stepped at the sudden movement and shout. Still Burr's shot was quick and accurate. Instead of tagging flesh, however, it sang off the receiver of Dancer's Winchester, sending the bullet whining off into the trees as the rifle went spinning from his hand.

A scream came from the porch of the house as the shot rang out.

Dancer yanked on Washoe's reins and the big gray horse reared up as John pawed past the skirt of his black rain slicker and found the walnut grips of his own .44 Colt. Jason triggered off a second shot. His target blocked by the towering bulk of Washoe, Burr's second shot was nevertheless again too close.

His bullet caught stirrup leather beneath Dancer's crippled foot with a nasty slapping sound.

Dancer's Colt was in his hand and he fired deliberately as Washoe came down to all fours and braced. John Dancer's shot caught Burr directly in the heart. Burr's eyes reflected amazement. His mouth formed a puzzled grin. The palomino swung away in panic and raced toward the yard of the ranch house, Burr clinging to his running horse, swaying like a rag doll in the saddle.

The rain still drove down in torrents. On the porch of the house Cassandra Blythe stood with her hands to her mouth. Her evil eyes caught sight of Dancer and she let loose a stream of shrill, savage curses as Jason Burr slumped from the saddle and fell to the rain-pooled earth not far from where Jared Fine still lay face up in the ooze.

Thunder rumbled, but the berserk

curses of Cassandra Blythe sounded clearly above it. She rushed off the porch, slipped and fell to hands and knees. She rose again, stumbling and sliding, rushing to the unmoving body of Jason Burr. She lifted his head as if to cradle it, but then began to slap at it violently, furiously, as if he too had let her down. Dancer watched without speaking from Washoe's back.

Crazed eyes rose up to meet his through the rain. Cassandra Blythe's fine blonde hair was rainwashed, her pretty little white dress soaked through. Mud covered her hands, knees and elbows.

She screamed out again in uncontrollable wrath. Then she saw Burr's pistol, flung free as he fell, and she dove toward it through the fury of the rainstorm. From her knees she shot wildly at Dancer four times, before the cylinder was emptied.

Then she threw the gun away, buried her face in her muddy hands and began to cry. As Dancer continued to watch, she slowly spread her arms and looked up to him, her expression changing, softening, becoming some sort of entreaty to forgive, to understand, to help her . . .

Dancer turned Washoe away from the bad-luck range and rode out through the cold and blustery day, the woman's banshee cries eventually smothered by the thunder and cleansing rush of the bitter wind and constant falling rain.

★   ★   ★

The morning was clear and bright. There was not a puddle of water anywhere when Dancer again reached Brownsville. It might never have rained, never have stormed. With Washoe stabled up and under Toby Waller's care, John Dancer hobbled his way across the street to the hotel, where his entrance silenced the lobby.

Guy Travers, in shirtsleeves and red

suspenders looked up from his paper-work, eyes startled. John made his way to the hotel desk heavily and rested both hands on it.

'Will you be staying with us again, Mr Dancer?' Travers asked uneasily.

'No, it's just that I forgot something here,' John answered.

From the back room Tess Travers had appeared, her round face decorated with a genuine smile. 'Hello, John,' she said. 'Is there something we can do for you?'

'Man says he left something behind,' Guy Travers said. 'Did you check . . . ?'

Tess's smile deepened. She under-stood if her husband did not. 'Sadie's in her room, John. Go on up.'

The staircase was a challenge. John figured he would have to get himself a cane and learn how to use it. He managed the fifty feet down the corridor to Sadie Fairchild's door easily but then found himself unable to complete what he had come to do just as he started to knock. He hesitated, thought about turning away and just leaving.

The small voice from within the room said: 'I'm here, John. Do come in.'

As he entered, he saw the chestnut-haired girl with those sad green eyes standing at the window. A light breeze fluttered the white curtains. She turned slowly toward him, her small hands clasped together. 'I recognized Washoe half a mile away. I've been watching, hoping you'd come by to see me. Are you back to stay, John?'

'No,' he said, taking two steps nearer. Her eyes grew a little sadder. 'I'm leaving again. As soon as Washoe's back in top shape.'

'Oh?' Sadie's eyes were on the tips of her shoes. 'Where will you go, John?'

'I don't know,' he said, shaking his head. 'Nor do I know what I will do once I get there. I only know the sort of place I want to find.'

'Do you, John?' Sadie's eyes lifted to his now. 'Where might that be?'

He told her.

'Where a man can live a full life, a rewarding life, without his gun. Without carving his own path to Hell.'

She smiled faintly, surprised and pleased that he had remembered her own words. Dancer shifted uncomfortably and braced himself, placing one hand on the post of her brass bed.

'Sadie . . . ?'

She waited as he hesitated. His eyes shifted down and away like a shy schoolboy's.

'When I leave . . . I know all about the things, the bad things that happened to you when you were young and your parents brought you across the prairie. I know that's why you stayed in Brownsville . . . ' He took a deep breath and tried it again.

'Now . . . do you think that now you would be brave enough to ride out onto the wide land, to leave this place?'

The sadness in her green eyes had vanished. They sparkled now with a sort

KNIFE EDGE

Tyler Hatch

Brad Winters, ramrod of the Block F ranch, only wants to do his job. However, his boss Matt Farrell has other ideas: he wants to re-enact the Battle of Hashknife Ridge, which had been fought there fifteen years earlier. It means a meeting of North and South — and old hatreds are far from buried. Before the battle begins there are shootings, robberies and assassination attempts. And by the time it's over, the wonder is that there is anybody left alive.

ONCE A RANGER

Hank J. Kirby

'Once a ranger, always a ranger' — so the saying went. But when Clint Taggart left under pressure, he was never happier. Then tragedy struck and the rangers wanted him back. Against his better judgement, he agreed and found his life and that of his remaining family in unimaginable danger: up against the biggest threat Texas had ever seen! But he still retained the old Ranger training, and Clint rode to meet his enemies head-on, determined to face the consequences.

Other titles in the
Linford Western Library:

JUDGE COLT PRESIDES

George J. Prescott

When one of the powerful Ducane family is hanged for murder in a border town, his father wipes out the place in revenge. Deputy Federal Marshal Fargo Reilly goes south to dispense justice and becomes involved in a gun-running conspiracy, and a plot to murder the president of Mexico. Reilly and his deputy Matt Crane fight to destroy the gang. But can Reilly also stop them from ransacking the nearby town of Perdition, where *Judge Colt Presides?*

BLUEGRASS BOUNTY

Jack Reason

The most wanted gunman and outlaw this side of the Rockies, Jude Lovell, is about to hang in the town of Saracen. The crowds flock to be at the event of the century. But Marshal Brand is deeply suspicious. Why are there so many of Lovell's gang gathered in the town? Have they come to mourn, or to stage a daring rescue? When the awful truth dawns it wreaks a devastating toll of death and destruction.

We do hope that you have enjoyed reading this large print book.

Did you know that all of our titles are available for purchase?

We publish a wide range of high quality large print books including:
Romances, Mysteries, Classics
General Fiction
Non Fiction and Westerns

Special interest titles available in large print are:
The Little Oxford Dictionary
Music Book, Song Book
Hymn Book, Service Book

Also available from us courtesy of Oxford University Press:
Young Readers' Dictionary
(large print edition)
Young Readers' Thesaurus
(large print edition)

For further information or a free brochure, please contact us at:
Ulverscroft Large Print Books Ltd.,
The Green, Bradgate Road, Anstey,
Leicester, LE7 7FU, England.
Tel: (00 44) **0116 236 4325**
Fax: (00 44) **0116 234 0205**

of bright temerity. Sadie stepped forward and tilted her head back to gaze up at him, her arms around his waist.

'With you, John Dancer,' she said, 'I would go anywhere.'

THE END